PUSHING UP POSIES

NEW YORK TIMES BESTSELLING AUTHOR
EVE LANGLAIS

E-ISBN: 978 177 384 153 3

Print ISBN: 978 177 384 154 0

FOREWORD

Lucifer's got his hands full with the Antichrist and another baby on its way. Add in a very pregnant and demanding Mother Earth, plus another prophecy about the end of the world and it's clear he needs to delegate more.

What he also needs? More minions to fill the ranks in his legion. With Cupid on a sabbatical and fewer babies being born than ever, he has to take drastic action.

Say hello to Grim Dating, a service dedicated to pairing humans with things that go bump in the night or hide under the bed. And who better to run this newly created department but some underworked Canadian Grim Reapers.

LUCIFER IS BACK WITH A DEVILISH NEW PLAN.

I should torture someone. Maybe have them tied to the rack and stretched until their limbs pop.

Been there. Done that.

A thousand times multiplied by a thousand more.

Just like he'd indulged in his share of hanging, beating, nailing, flailing, dunking, and more...

After awhile, the screams of those he punished lost all meaning. Seriously, extreme pain brought the language that spewed from those he tortured to an incomprehensible level. Argh. Agh. Wah. How was he supposed to understand that?

Some accused him of not caring, not understanding, yet Lucifer knew pain. Had suffered so much of it. He'd first truly felt the agony when he was cast from Heaven. Betrayed most cruelly. Wings torn from him. Banned from the only home he knew and thrust into a hot Hades filled with mindless beasts, sent there to die.

And for what?

A question he knew better than to ask. Yet, much like Eve later did after his seduction of her in the garden, some things couldn't be ignored. He'd just wanted an answer.

Lucifer stopped his pacing to stare at a painting of a child, a small and slender lad. What the humans would call a teen, fresh faced and soft. A boy who still trusted as he knelt, staring at the sun, his hands clasped in prayer, asking a simple question. The image captured the moment before everything changed.

Only a few words that, even now, he couldn't bear to think of. Because those words saw him banned. Cast off to basically die alone.

But that was a million years ago, and he'd survived despite it all. He'd evolved since that time, as had the Hell he'd been banished to. Few people knew, and even fewer recalled, that when Lucifer arrived in this dimension, a strange pocket of reality, the ground was frozen solid, a world encased in a veneer of ice. Everything paused. Waiting.

For its king.

Within the first few breaths of his arrival, he'd almost died. Then again, that first day. Week. Month. Year. Every day he'd fought. Every day he'd gotten stronger. It helped he wasn't completely alone.

There were demons in this place. And spirits. Magic, too. A lonely castoff found companionship where he could. Lucifer taught the demons to speak and think. When that got boring, he created new species. Minions to surround him, none of them gentle or kind.

That was a long time ago. He'd gotten more discerning since then. It helped he eventually found a way to visit the human realm. Saw all the wandering souls. The ones heaven rejected, caught in limbo.

Lucifer snared them all. The ones too far gone, who didn't remember their humanity, went right into the abyss, a hole in his realm that went farther than he dared explore. It would be thousands of years before he'd realize it recycled souls. But at the time, it provided a place to toss the most lost of the ghosts.

Over time, and with a little help from Eve's descendants, humans became truly sentient. Why he remembered the first time he had a conversation with one. Grnrg had evolved quite a bit since his Neanderthal days.

Over time, Hell became populated, filling with souls, drawing Heaven's attention. His brother— who'd decided he would be the one God—had initially seemed pleased to find his long-thought-dead brother, Lucifer.

A lie. Funny how Elyon—the name his brother had chosen for this epoch, though he'd been formerly known for a short time as Bob—got away with not telling the , but none of the souls entering his paradise could. Heaven rejected souls for the slightest of sins.

Over time, a competition evolved between him and Elyon. How could it not? The golden older brother who always had their creator's blessing. Unlike Lucifer, cast down, unwelcome.

Now a king of something bigger.

As a ruler he had subjects. So many bloody souls and demons and other things that sometimes wanted to be called gods. Lucifer thought it was cute when Zeus and the others blustered about, showing their almighty strength. The weakened Greek gods no longer enjoyed the worshipping power that used to feed their strength.

I could crush them like bugs.

Lucifer didn't need people to believe in him, although he did enjoy the adulation. He had existed long before the humans took over as sentient life. At times he missed the simplicity of the life led by dolphins, but they were chatty things and, for some reason, turned into sea monsters when they died and got reborn in Hell. The Styx was running amok with them, what with all the pollution these days.

A knock at the door made him stiffen. The painting of the child—that pathetic twat—flipped and became a hellscape full of fire and damnation as befitted a dark king of his stature. Screw those that would call him prince.

He was the one and only leader of Hell. While he'd fathered many, all but a few had died. Usually by his hand when they came after his throne.

I don't know what I'm doing wrong. He'd tried raising his children differently. Taking a hands-off approach with some. They ended up with daddy issues and tried to kill him.

Others of his progeny got a chance to live in the castle with him. No matter what he did, they eventually reached an age where they came after him. Sometimes with tears as they held their weapon over his chest, only to realize within moments they couldn't kill him so easily.

In a few cases, it had hurt him when he had to act in return. Sometimes he mourned the deaths by not making any children for a century or two. But inevitably, the urge would rise to see himself in a smaller replica that would evolve. To teach someone of his blood. To perhaps finally find a child worthy of his throne.

That child wasn't Bambi, who strutted into his

5

office, wearing an inappropriate-length skirt and a crop top that showed off her bellybutton. Not that she had a bellybutton, just a jewel pierced into the flesh. Unlike his other living children, Bambi wasn't born of a woman's womb.

"Dark Lord"—she paused and gave him a sassy salute—"I heard you requested my presence."

"Three days ago!" he barked. While he'd always hidden his pride in her loose morals, he couldn't abide her new sassy manner.

"Are you sure it wasn't like thirty minutes? Because that's when Muriel told me to get my butt over here."

Muriel, his other daughter. The one most like and least like him. His pride and joy. There was no point in pretending he didn't have a favorite. His new son might eventually take the spot, but right now, he still shit his pants. "Where is your irritating sister?"

"Right here, Daddy." Muriel suddenly shimmered into view.

A lesser man might have grabbed his chest and exclaimed about his heart. Good thing Lucifer had it removed and hidden in a new spot. Not even his wife knew where he'd stashed it.

His youngest had gotten good at wielding her magic. A mix of not just Hell and Earth from her mom and dad but also hints of other elements.

Blame her different-flavored husbands. Each one enhanced her magic in a new way.

At times he envied his daughter and her harem. Then he inwardly flinched as he imagined Gaia punishing him for the thought.

"Where have you been?" he snapped. "I've been waiting." Waiting was for those not trying to run a Hell with a bajillion citizens. Not to mention, the Devil should never wait for anyone.

Muriel appeared as lean as ever and mean looking, too. She'd chosen to wear form-fitting jeggings, molded to her skin and cinching in at the waist. She wore a light blouse, ankle boots, and a sword down her spine. A stylish girl like her father. "I was busy. You know, motherhood, being a wife to four guys, and dating a fifth."

His eyebrows tried to escape his face. "A fifth? Since when?"

"Since a few weeks ago," was Muriel's coy reply.

"And you only tell me now?" How did he not know his daughter entertained yet another mate? Each one made her stronger. Eventually she'd reach a point he'd have to act. Killing a husband or two would reduce her power base, but she'd be pissed when she found out. And inevitably she would. He'd had it happen so many times before, and yet, what other choice did he have? Let her become more powerful than him?

He was too selfish to allow that.

"I haven't told anyone because I was checking to see how he fit with my men first. If they approve, then I'll probably marry him."

"That's quite the reverse harem. Kind of jelly," Bambi declared.

"You were once dating a whole hockey team," Muriel pointed out.

"Yeah, but none of them ever married me, and I got tired of dealing with their jilted partners."

"Next time just kill them. It saves the hassle." The advice came from experience, yet his girls both exclaimed.

"Really, Daddy," Muriel chided. "That seems unnecessary."

"So is rubbing my face in the fact you're living your best life with your harem. It's cruel and unusual punishment."

Muriel smirked as she perched on his desk. "I know. What can I say? I learned to torture from the best."

The disrespect was an homage to her parentage. "Keep irritating me, and I will abdicate and name you my heir again," he threatened.

It still surprised him that when he'd had his mental lapse and Muriel had taken over, she'd not kept the job. She'd handed it back the moment he'd recovered.

It made no sense. All his children eventually betrayed him for the throne of Hell. But Muriel actually dumped it into his lap and then spent weeks after checking on him, making sure he wasn't about to leave the ruling of the kingdom in her hands. It had to be a ploy. He just couldn't decipher yet how it worked in her favor.

"Don't you dare try and give me your shitty-ass job," Muriel huffed, hopping off the desk. "I will drag you back kicking and screaming if you try."

"I'll do it." Bambi raised her hand. She'd flung herself into the club chair facing his desk, legs over the armrest, almost showing off her cookie, looking like a whore.

The pride welling in him wasn't enough to distract from his annoyance. "You are not ready to run Hell."

His eldest pouted. "You gave it to Muriel once, and she's younger than me."

"Never again!" Muri declared. "You don't want it either, sis."

"I want to run something." Bambi crossed her arms and almost fell out of her shirt. Just like her mother, who'd once fallen on his cock. He still maintained it wasn't his fault he came. None of his three girlfriends at the time had any sympathy for him.

"What about that brothel you own?" the Devil pointed out.

"I sold it because it was boring."

"If you're bored, have sex," Lucifer suggested. It always fixed him.

I wish. It's been ages since I've screwed anyone." Rouged lips turned down.

"I find that hard to believe," Muriel muttered.

That made two of them. Bambi's mother had been a succubus, killed by a human while she was feeding. Bambi hadn't been even two digits old. In a rare gesture of respect, he'd hired the best madams Hell had to offer to teach his daughter about her mother's heritage as the most highly paid whore. He'd done his job so well his daughter held records. Slut of the Year. Whore of the Decade. He knew her mother, Mitzy, would be so proud.

"I'm abstaining so that I can make it special with someone." Bambi might as well have dropped a bomb. Her words had an explosive effect.

Muriel's eyes widened. "Holy shit, you're in love."

"Lust," Bambi corrected. "But War won't come near me if he thinks I've been with other men."

"I can't believe you're still seeing him. And making such a sacrifice. He must be pretty special." Muriel clasped her hands.

"I am dying to see what's under that armor of his." Bambi fanned herself.

Lucifer's stomach heaved. "Can we stop with this mushy shit? I am going to barf."

"Is this a bad time to say I love you, Daddy?" Muriel batted her lashes.

"What is wrong with you, saying that kind of crap?" He shook his finger at her, and overhead, thunder cracked. He'd been having more lapses lately. Too much stress. Not enough sex.

And given the very pregnant Gaia gave him the stink eye every time he glanced in her direction, that drought wouldn't end any time soon.

"You're the best father a girl could ask for. And an awesome granddaddy, too." Muriel just kept going. The compliments over the top and turning into a mockery he could handle better than the emotional shit.

He snorted. "One day, I'm going to kill you for that insolence." He'd be sad when that day came.

"Only if I don't kill you first, Daddy," Muriel sang, and winked.

Muri had no idea she wasn't the one he needed to worry about. The enemy that would truly challenge him had yet to be born...but it wouldn't be long now. He had to prepare.

"Stop jibbering and jabbering. We are in a crisis, my daughters. A threat like you cannot imagine." He flung an arm and wished he'd worn his cape. It would have added the necessary dramatic effect. At least the rest of him appeared regal. His black Hessian boots—taken from the body of a soldier on a battlefield before the blood had cooled—shone. His breeches were tucked into the tops of them and molded his firm thighs. Firmer than they'd been in centuries given the amount of nights he'd paced, bouncing his baby boy who wouldn't sleep unless his daddy walked him. A child with the shittiest timing.

One second the kid was asleep in his crib, snoring through the damned monitor Gaia insisted they keep in the bedroom, but the moment Lucifer fondled his wife...

"Wah!"

And guess who got to get up since Gaia was hugely pregnant? It was his own fault, as she reminded him on a daily basis.

Even his dreams weren't safe from his cock-blocking son. Fall into a nice dream where he was chasing wenches? The crying was usually accompanied by the smelliest diaper. And could he snap his fingers and clean up the mess?

Oh no, Gaia insisted they care for the child themselves. Like mere servants. No wonder people had lost respect for the lord of hell. A glorified nursemaid.

"Slow down there, Daddy. You're going to wear a hole in the floor you're pacing so hard. Calm your nerves and take slow, deep breaths."

He paused and glared. "Are you placating me?"

"Mocking, actually." Muriel winked.

Apparently having a harem of men didn't curb her of disrespect. Perhaps he should send more discipline videos for her husbands to study. He had recorded an entire collection.

"I will gladly kill you when the time comes, but today is not that day. Take a look at this." He swept his hand at the recreation of Hell, a diorama painstakingly created by a team of building block engineers. The detail was incredible.

"Playing with toys again?" Muriel teased, but she did stand closer to it.

Bambi slinked over to the table with the demolished blocks tumbled all over. "What happened here?" She ran a finger through the rubble.

How to explain that while he'd been plotting the demise of the mortal plane Junior had crawled over and demanded Lucifer pick him up. The baby, though, didn't want his father's arms but the contents of the table. Watching Junior trample the world, crushing the human armies and waving his arms as he exclaimed, "Bow, peasants!" had Lucifer beaming in pride.

No point in letting the lad know that it most likely would not be him eventually leading the armies of darkness. The boy wouldn't be seasoned enough. But Muri and her husband generals would be just right. Maybe he wouldn't kill any of them yet. The prophecy did say something about the lamb arriving with her ten herders. Yet there was also the prediction in the ancient sea scroll he'd stolen that didn't mention him with any of his daughters by his side.

He'd not told anyone about the prophecies he'd been collecting. Some secrets were for the devil alone.

"Ignore the broken blocks. That tableau isn't important. I need you to look at this rendition of Hell. More specifically, the fourth ring." The soldiers' ring. Where his legion lived and learned before getting stationed to other rings to serve and protect the realm.

"What about it?" Muriel asked, swirling her finger amidst a battalion, knocking them over.

"What you're looking at are the current recruits."

It was Bambi who said it first. "Doesn't seem like you have as many this year."

"Less even than last year. With a prediction it will get worse. People aren't having little demons like they used to. Fewer and fewer damned are signing up to fight in my service," Lucifer railed.

"You're exaggerating. I'm sure it will get better. Put out some more recruiting posters. Improve the pay and benefits. You should be happy no one wants to sign up. It's the best indication of a prosperous kingdom. You don't need a big army in times of peace." Muriel just had to make him feel even worse.

"It is exactly because of that peace that we do! Complacency leads to fewer numbers. Fewer numbers weakens us. And that is when the enemy steps in." Did she think him new at this? He'd not ruled Hell this long by ignoring the signs.

"I think you're overreacting," Muriel stubbornly insisted. "Sure, the numbers are a little down. Blame that mini war with Lilith that decimated the ranks."

Lilith had been powering some spells using the damned. He'd lost too many before they'd managed to destroy her.

"I guess it didn't help that we then had that problem with Ursula when she escaped from that prison dimension," Bambi reminded. Most of the ninth ring had perished when the seas rose and covered the land.

"Double whammy," he agreed. "And not as bad as others Hell has gone through. In the past we've always recovered. But this time is different."

"Why?" Muri asked.

"Because someone has been spreading free condoms throughout my Legion." Unprotected sex. It was practically a rule. Fornicate and if someone got pregnant, then Hell gained a new volunteer.

"Don't look at me. I would never give out condoms. I hate the feel of rubber in my cavern of unholy acts." Bambi shrugged, and Lucifer knew if he'd been any other man, she would have let her shirt slip and show off a nip.

Chip off the old slut block, she was. She and her sister Muriel. Hard to believe his youngest, who once spouted she'd only lose her virginity to love, was now courting a fifth member for her harem. He'd have been happier if she was using that jizz cocktail to make super-grandbabies. Unfortunately, Muriel was having issues with her womanly parts. Something about Lilith fucking her right up when she'd stolen Lucille, his first granddaughter.

"Condoms, the shots, and that bloody morning-after pill are ruining my plans for world domination!" Hell and Earth had both been seeing lower birth rates since contraception became widespread. And as for abortion... Not one of those fledgling souls ended up in hell. Meaning they'd gone straight to heaven. What could those angels—led by his nephew Charlie—be doing with all those teeny tiny souls?

"What are you talking about? Evil acts are up. People are sinning more than ever. Why they say the 2020s will probably be the turning point where divorces outweigh marriage. Think of all those people fornicating and living in sin," Muri declared.

"But they're not making babies, Muri! My legion is only at a fraction of what it used to be. For the first time in eons, the rings have stopped growing. We actually have room for everyone. Or did you not notice the ninth ring and the space beyond it?" He pointed at the Wilds, represented as a sheet of darkness because few went and returned. Mapping wasn't possible because it was ever changing.

"What's happening?" Muriel frowned as her gaze tracked over the space he indicated.

"What you are seeing is a shrinkage of the ninth ring. By all accounts, the Wilds are closing in."

"Eating the ring?" Muriel gasped.

"Doing something to it. No way yet to stop it. No way of knowing if it will cease before reaching the eighth."

"What of the people living in the ninth? The animals? What's happening to them once the Wilds take over their strip?" Bambi asked, pointing to a small village in the encroaching black wave's way.

"No idea. I've yet to get a proper report back. It would seem agents sent into the Wilds aren't returning at the moment."

"Oh shit. That's no good."

"If only my most experienced tracker, who's been beyond the ninth ring, could find out what is happening."

Muriel glared. "You are not sending Teivel into that death trap. Have Nef cast a spell or something." Nef being Nefertiti, his ancient sorceress.

"What a great idea, because we didn't try scrying first." She deserved the sarcastic retort.

"Didn't you just say Hell had room again?" Muri mused aloud. "Could be that we're shrinking because of the decrease in numbers. Might be that it will stop when we reach a point of balance?"

"We've been balanced for almost two thousand years. I know the signs. We're about to head into a tipping point." Those were never good. During one of them, his brother had a temper tantrum and drowned almost the entire population on Earth. All those new souls arriving in Hell tied up his ability to pursue other things for decades. Then, just as he caught up, there was that skirmish in South America. The Inca knew how to wage a proper war.

"You think the world is tipping in Heaven's favor?" Muriel shook her head. "Impossible. We totally outnumber them. You know getting past the pearly gates takes a perfect record."

"I am well aware of the criteria; a clean soul, without a blemish." He couldn't help thinking of those who supported abortion. Little did they know they were doing his brother's work. Releasing souls before they had a chance to become imperfect by sinning.

How many millions now? Hell had been building its numbers for a long time; however, Lilith's attack, not to mention attrition, had put a serious dent in them.

"How do you propose we fix this supposed imbalance?" Muriel asked, more than a little sarcastically.

"I'm going to need more souls. More demons. More everything, or we're doomed."

2

WHAT'S A DEVIL HAVE TO DO TO GET SOME RESPECT?

LUCIFER'S PRONOUNCEMENT ECHOED, and yet Muri didn't appear impressed. Even Bambi rolled her eyes.

The disrespect had him huffing smoke. "Is there a problem? I don't see either of you looking worried."

"Because you also claimed we were doomed last week when you couldn't find your other ducky sock."

"It was my fanged duck sock for your information. Special order, and I needed it to complete my outfit." People expected a certain level of style from him these days. Every day he posted images of his ensemble on Hellagram, Hellbook, and other places. The people needed to see their king looking his best.

Muri didn't appear swayed. "What about the week before when you said everyone would die after the kitchen informed you of a hellberry shortage caused by the Hell-freezing-over issue that killed off most of the bushes."

"Everyone almost did die. You know I need my pie."

"What about three months ago when you said Hell was doomed if you didn't get tickets to the Backstreet Boys reunion concert?" Bambi was next to pile on.

"I might have exaggerated a little bit." He squeezed his fingers. In his defense, Backstreet Boys was one of his finer accomplishments.

Muri snorted. "You are the devil who cries apocalypse all the time. It's hard to believe you."

Lucifer turned serious. "The lack of minions *is* serious."

"I thought you were handling it with your super-duper matchmaking skills. Aren't you responsible for like dozens of hookups? Remy and Ysabel, Katie and that serious dude who skulks around, Charon's boy and stuff?"

"Yes, yes. Blah. Blah. I got them knocking boots and there will hundreds more banging by the time the Hell on the High Seas cruises take off. But it's not enough. We need more minions, which is why it's time to infiltrate the mortal plane."

Muri's eyes widened. "You mean pair your demons with humans to create super babies?"

He nodded. "Yes, except I cannot send my

demons in any great numbers to the mortal plane without you-know-who noticing." He eyed the ceiling and wondered what his nephew Charlie was up to. Ever since he'd taken over from Lucifer's brother, Charlie had gone silent. While the souls that made it to the gates of heaven appeared to be getting inside, no one was coming out. Nor was there any news.

What did his nephew plot? Him and those damned angels. And what of Elyon? No one had heard from him since the angels took him into custody at his granddaughter's birthday party.

"Sending demons up top is a bad idea. You'd be better off bringing some humans to Hell instead," Muri suggested.

Bambi finally took an interest in the conversation. "Have you forgotten the air is bad for their lungs?" Hell and its constantly falling ash wasn't healthy for carbon-based creatures.

"Daddy could build them a habitat."

"I could, but that seems like a lot of work for me, and the whole point was to delegate. No, the best plan is for my most valuable minions to head to the mortal plane to plant some seeds."

"Send demons with orders to fuck humans and no one to keep an eye on them?" Muri recapped in a low drawl. "Gee, I wonder how that could go wrong. First off, you do realize that people are going to notice if a demon with horns and hooves is walking around?"

"Not necessarily. I've seen some of the new clothing trends out there," Lucifer remarked. "And besides, they'd obviously wear a glamour."

"Not all of your minions are compatible with mortals."

"Then they don't get to go." Seemed obvious to him.

"Who gets to decide that? Not to mention they'll be pissed if they're not chosen," Muri argued.

"I'll give them hellgrog to drown their troubles." He waved a hand. "We will only send our most likely to impregnate and tell them to get busy."

"You can't tell them that!" Muriel shrieked. "Women have rights now, you know."

"Meaning men don't?" He rubbed his chin. "Maybe I'll just send female demons then."

"That's not what I meant," his youngest daughter huffed. "You can't just open a portal to Earth and send your minions over with instructions to get someone pregnant."

"Muri has a point. Demons and many others that are used to Hell's more lax laws might get into trouble if let loose. Their antics could very well draw *his* attention."

All three of them eyed the ceiling, even though heaven wasn't technically above.

"Who said there won't be rules? Freedom isn't the ultimate evil, after all. It's clauses with subclauses." He rubbed his hands. "There will also be a submission process. With a test. And a physical."

"And? They still need someone to monitor them to make sure they don't step out of line," Muriel pointed out.

"Obviously, which is why they'll be overseen."

"By whom? You were just whining your legion was too small."

The mention of the S word in his presence made him want to whip out his dick and prove otherwise, but these were his daughters. Even he had some boundaries.

"The legion is needed here, but we do have another underutilized group."

"Who?" Muri asked, curiosity in the word.

"You might have heard about our overabundance of reapers." His fault. He'd transformed so many of them when it appeared as if that bird flu would eradicate a good chunk of the population. However, at the last minute, his brother tweaked the virus and saved the world. As if to compound that insult, none of the countries had yet committed to engaging in a world war. Stupid peace talks.

All those people staying alive left him with too many soul takers, beings meant to act as guides to the freshly departed, ensuring they ended up in

Hades where they belonged. The sixth ring with its many reaper guilds was bulging with the currently unemployed.

"You're going to stud out your reapers?" Bambi asked with a finely arched brow.

"Yes. And no. I was thinking of encouraging their contact with humans but also using them to scout viable subjects that might be useful copulation partners for some of my demons that aren't interested in settling down." Most demons thought monogamy was torture. He'd heard the whispers behind his back wondering how the Dark Lord, the most sexually prolific of them all, could stand being with one woman. After all, he'd coined the term sex addict.

What they didn't know was Gaia could become any woman—or man—and had an ability to clone herself that any superhero would envy. Roleplaying kept their sex life spicy.

"Sounds like you want to start up a grim dating service," Bambi joked.

"As a matter of fact, I do, and I want you and Muri to be in charge of it."

3

THE GLOOM PROVED palpable in the Grim Guild. Hundreds of reapers, sitting around long trestle tables, doing fuck all. It led to more than a few fights, and Brody let it happen. He'd long ago given up on disciplining them for blowing off steam. Quite frankly, at times, Brody wanted to join them in hitting something.

Two centuries since he'd been put in charge. Over half a century since they'd had any real work.

The crew was bored and lacking direction. It had gotten so bad some of the reapers had even chosen to go to their final deaths by throwing themselves into the abyss—a bottomless hole at the center of Hell where souls could go to be recycled. Although Brody did have to wonder if the whole recycling thing was true. After all, no one could actually confirm it happened. Souls reborn in bodies on the mortal plane didn't remember their past lives, no matter what a certain religion claimed.

Sitting on his platform, overlooking a guild once mighty, Brody sighed. What would it take to get them busy again? To knock the dust off their cloaks, the dull off their scythes, and put a glide in their step? Would someone stop screwing around and launch that biological weapon! A nuclear meltdown would be epic. Or as his lieutenant, Julio, suggested when drunk one boring night, what if all the wind turbines in a certain province suddenly ripped around and went scything across the land?

Personally, he thought their next best bet would be an ice storm that knocked out power during a deep freeze that lasted for days or, if lucky, weeks.

Without a knock or any warning, the massive double doors were flung open, slamming into the reapers standing guard. They were smooshed into the wall behind the portal. Only the edges of their robes peeked out as Hell's biggest slut entered.

"It's Bambi." The appearance of Lucifer's oldest daughter was an honor that had many stirring and straightening their hoods. Everyone recognized Bambi, even the guild commander. Not that Brody had ever partaken of her services, but he knew many in this room who'd had the carnal delight. Seen the videos, too. If he weren't so depressed, she might have even tempted a known celibate like Brody.

Although, if he were to indulge, it wouldn't be inside the guild. Only reapers were allowed within the guild walls. Bambi surely knew that, so why the fuck did she strut through the Grim Guild as if she owned it? More than a few gazes undressed her, not that there was much to strip. Her dress made it clear undergarments were not included.

A few reapers dropped hands to their laps for a less-than-discreet tug, which got them slapped by their feminine counterparts. Except for Karina. She had her hand shoved down her pants as far as any of her grim brothers.

Given Bambi appeared to be heading for him, Brody shoved off his seat and circled his empty desk. As grim leader for the Canadian branch, he managed one of the least busy reaper guilds. Fucking Canadians hadn't had a good war since the 1940s. Although they'd seen a slight uptick in 2019 from distracted driving, that wouldn't last. Already the government was passing strict laws that would curb that deadly habit.

Spoilsports.

"What do you want?" Brody barked, standing on the edge of his platform and glaring at her.

"Well, aren't you just a ray of sunshine, big boy." She stopped below him and winked.

"This is the Grim Guild. You don't belong here."

"Actually, I do. Orders from the big man himself. You know, the guy I call Daddy." She smirked as she held out a rolled scroll.

"What the fuck is that?" Was he being summoned? Would the Dark Lord fire him for not bringing in the numbers? Not his fault the Canadians wouldn't die. At least when they did, most were polite about it.

"I'm going to Hell?"

"Yes."

"So kind of you to come and escort me."

Bambi waggled the scroll. "Consider this document your new mission statement."

"My what? Give me that." He reached for the scroll, but she tucked it behind her back.

Bambi tsked and shook her head. "Not so quick, big boy. First you're going to give me a hand up there."

"This is the commander's platform. Only me or my lieutenants are allowed on it." Not entirely true, but he was loath to have the woman joining him. He had a bad feeling in his gut, as bad as the one he got when the war ended and peace was declared.

"Would this be the moment I'm supposed to tell you that I'm your new overlady? Because I am. Well, me and my sister. But Muri said she'd handle things on her side while I take care of matters in Hell.

Which means you and this guild." She beamed a saucy smile enhanced by a wink.

"Like fuck."

"No thanks. I'm currently abstaining from casual sex as I'm seeing someone. You might know him. Fellow called War? Stubborn guy. Won't even hold my hand. But I like a man playing hard to get. Makes it all the sweeter when he becomes mine." Her smile turned sly.

"Why don't you go bang this boyfriend of yours and leave me to do my job."

"Alas, my sex life will have to wait. I'm here to fix your guild."

"Unless your boyfriend is going to start a war, then you're wasting my time."

"Actually, you're wasting mine." Suddenly her mien went from playful to serious with a hint of annoyed. A tiny spark danced in the depths of her eyes, a reminder of her heritage. "My father trusted me with a job and gave me your guild to accomplish it. If you think you're going to get in my way…" She didn't finish the threat. She didn't have to. Everyone knew the consequences of defying the Dark Lord's wishes.

"Fucking fine. Get up here so we can talk without so many curious ears," he growled.

"I thought you'd never ask, big boy." She half

turned and snapped her fingers. "You and you, give me a boost."

Two of his taller guild members stood and cupped their hands. When she stepped into them, they lifted her within reach of Brody, who had no choice. He held out his hand, grasped her slender one in his, and hauled her to his level. He used to have a ladder, but given he could float, when it got borrowed, he didn't bother replacing it.

Bambi stepped into his office and cast around a quick glance. "This won't do at all."

"Excuse me?"

"I'll need to call my interior designer. Because that"—she pointed to the far corner with its pallet —"is not a bed. I need something with some springs and a pillow top, not to mention, where is the color? I'm thinking a bit of pink to liven it up. Maybe some flowers. And incense."

"There is nothing wrong with my guild."

"Says you." Her nose wrinkled. "I'm all for the scent of people perspiring from work, but I draw the line at the unwashed masses. What happened to your place?"

Shame struck Brody. He almost ducked his head. "Death isn't a booming business, not for us anyway. I don't suppose the Dark Lord is planning to rectify that? Maybe his wife could throw a devastating natural disaster to help boost the morale of my crew." He swept a hand, noticing they had the attention of most of the members. They just couldn't hear anything spoken. His office had a cocoon of silence keeping their words private.

"I've got good news and bad news. The good news is you're about to become super busy."

"Really? What's the bad?"

"You're no longer going to be collecting souls for my father."

"Oh. Then what will we be doing?" Perhaps they'd become part of the legion. An elite fighting force. A—

"What?" He surely misunderstood her next words.

"I said, you're about to become the director of the brand-new and exciting Grim Dating Guild," Bambi exclaimed.

"I don't understand." He truly didn't.

"Read the letter. It explains everything."

Except it didn't. Parts of it stuck out, such as "… *you are to facilitate the meeting of those deemed proper mating material with humans. You may also fornicate at will. The more babies, the better…*" There was the Dark Lord's confirmation that, indeed, Bambi and Muriel were to be his new Guild supervisors instead of Mictain, the ancient Aztec death god who'd taken over when the last supervisor went a little crazy and recycled himself into the abyss.

The letter also made it clear Brody wasn't being demoted. On the contrary, he would still be a leader with all his reapers below him. His Canadian department would be swallowed by the American guild and become a massive North American one. Brody and his men would create a new kind of guild with the possibility of growing if they did well, with one big caveat. "We're going to the mortal plane?"

"Tada! Exciting, isn't it?" Bambi beamed. "You and your men will go topside to run the operation. I'll remain behind, coordinating the submission process and then sending you the eligible candidates."

It still made little sense. "You want us to communicate with humans?"

"Only if you have to. So long as you facilitate meetings—aka sexual hookups—your people can remain hiding in the background. Doesn't it sound exciting?"

More like a nightmare. Brody felt the beginnings of his first headache since he'd died and agreed to become a reaper. "When does the new job start?"

"Now. Your first task is to get an office ready to receive the first wave of horny demons. Here's your keys." She tossed a jangling ring at him. "If you have trouble with them, talk to the woman across the hall. Oh, and Brody?"

"What?"

"Have fun."

Before he could pack his things or even argue a bit more, Bambi shoved him. A portal opened, and just like when a soul was ready to cross, he felt a tugging that zipped him through an ether space of nothing and immensity before dropping him onto the mortal plane.

The new job started now.

4

Posie couldn't help but notice when the new neighbor moved in across the hall. For one, they arrived late in the evening, grumbling and stomping in the hall.

Rude.

She glared at the door, her glasses perched on the tip of her nose. She only wore them for reading. Darned paperbacks made the print too small these days.

"Fucking outrageous."

The curse drew her from the chair to the door. She peeked through her little peephole and blinked at the large form in the hall, an amorphous shape hidden beneath a floor-length cloak. The garment might have seemed odd if she didn't live above some gamers who role-played. She never saw them without their costumes. One fellow liked to wear a full-on white beard and wizard robes while yet another had pointed elf ears and bright green contacts. It still hadn't prepared her for the guy in the loincloth, carrying a big fake axe, who'd asked if she'd like to come in for a cup of tea. She was sure that was code for "become my buxom maiden in need of saving." The answer was no.

Posie not only didn't dress up for Halloween she was the furthest thing imaginable from the adventurous type. She was a boring secretary for a small law firm dealing in home sales and purchases.

Day in and out, she saw frazzled people nervously awaiting the paperwork that said they now owed banks for the next twenty some years or fist-pumped as they got away from those deadly monthly payments. Nothing even close to the excitement seen with fiery divorces or criminal cases.

Posie thought the people who signed their lives away to a bank were giving away money. Posie was perfectly happy renting. Let someone else deal with the maintenance and headaches, not to mention the upturns and downturns in the market. She didn't like change.

At all.

A new neighbor wasn't much change, but that depended on who moved in. Her last neighbor had been the perfect type. Rarely seen. Never speaking, only nodding if they happened to pass in the halls. She never would have imagined he was a serial arsonist who would die in one of the blazes he set. He didn't even smoke.

Returning to her chair, she tried to continue reading as the grumbling and thumping in the hall continued. Why so much noise?

By the time a firm knock came at her door, her annoyance had reached a fever pitch. It didn't improve when a glance through the peephole showed the hulking, cloaked figure.

She knew better than to open to a stranger or even pretend she was home. She said nothing.

"Hello?" A deep, rumbled query that she couldn't miss hearing.

She clamped her lips.

"Are you going to answer the door? I can hear you breathing." The rebuke was clearly masculine.

She slapped a hand over her mouth. He surely joked.

"Are all humans this annoying?" she could have sworn she heard him mumble. "Dammit, I'm not going to harm you. I require aid with the locking mechanism for my apartment." His odd style of speech held a hint of accent, almost but not quite British.

"I'm sorry but I can't help you," she finally replied.

"Of course, you can't," he drawled. "Isn't that just the fucking icing on a perfectly shitty day? Then again, why would I be surprised by this era? Everyone is too busy. Fucking self-absorbed assholes."

He kept muttering, and she pressed her eye to the peephole to see him at his door again, jiggling the key in the lock. Was it even the correct key?

Perhaps he wasn't a new neighbor after all but a robber. Should she call the police? They would want her to file a report and ask questions. Maybe even come inside her place and expect her to entertain them with coffee and donuts as they filled out paperwork.

Perish the thought.

On second thought, what kind of robber would knock and ask for help? Not to mention, it wasn't as if the empty apartment across the way held anything of value. The previous tenant had died, and once the police had finished fingerprinting and tagging items in his apartment, building management had it emptied and cleaned.

"Stupid lock." He kicked the door, and she winced.

She really shouldn't get involved. Really

shouldn't open the door and say, "These old locks sometimes stick. Let me try."

He whirled, the hood of his cloak still hiding his features. "I know how to use a fucking key. It doesn't work. That twat must have given me the wrong one."

Rude. A sexy voice that didn't match the bad attitude. Still, her good manners prevailed. "Let me see."

"Why? So you can agree that I know what the fuck I'm talking about?"

She pursed her lips. "You know what? Stay out in the hall. See if I care. You can explain it to the police when I call them." She went to whirl, only to hear him huff.

"I apologize. If you could provide assistance, it would be appreciated."

If he'd not been so polite, she might have ignored him. But...she couldn't do it. She sighed as she turned around. "Let's see what you've got."

He held out a gloved hand, a finger dangling a set of keys on a ring. The leather covering had her taking a step back. Didn't serial killers wear gloves?

He saw nothing amiss and jangled the ring. "It's got two. One is too small, and the other won't turn."

The keys actually appeared legitimate. She had an almost identical set. "The little one is for the mailbox." She held out her hand, and he dropped them into her palm. She didn't move to try them, though.

That would bring her too close to him. "Do you mind giving me some space?"

He took a step back. Not what she'd hoped for; however, she doubted asking him to stand at the other end of the hall would go over too well. She had to be careful to not let paranoia control her. Wearing a cloak and gloves didn't make him nefarious. Although he could be hiding any number of weapons in its folds.

She regretted coming out into the hall. The quicker she got the door unlocked, the faster she could escape him.

The key slid into the lock, and she yanked the handle to draw it tight against the jamb. She wrenched the key to the left, felt it catch. She pulled harder, and it finally clicked. Leaving the key in the lock, she opened the door and stepped away. "There you go."

"That was emasculating," he growled.

"The trick is to hold it tight, especially when it rains outside and the building gets damp."

She couldn't see his expression, but his entire posture scowled at the offending door. His tone was stiff as he said, "Thank you, ma'am."

She could have winced at the ma'am. At thirty-six, surely she wasn't that old. Still, it was a gesture of respect. "You're welcome. I guess you're the new neighbor." She could have winced at her lame attempt at polite talk.

"I am. Good evening."

And that was it. He went inside, shut the door, and left her staring at it. At least he wasn't the chatty type. Perhaps he wouldn't be a bad neighbor to have.

But she really hoped he got rid of that cloak. Because it was just plain creepy.

5

BRODY PRACTICALLY SLAMMED the door in the woman's face. No other choice given his embarrassment. A tiny woman had managed to open the door when a big strong reaper couldn't? He should hand in his balls now.

On a positive note, he'd accomplished his first mission. As he'd travelled through the ether from Hell to the mortal plane, the name and address of his victim—er, human potential for fornication—came to him.

Posie Ringwald. Apartment 5B, which happened to be across the hall from 5A. His new living quarters.

He stared around the dingy apartment, empty of furniture, not even a pallet. Not that he cared. He didn't plan to stay here long. Ousted from his office. Told this was a promotion. Maybe someone else would appreciate being dumped here to lead a special project for the Dark Lord. Not Brody.

He remembered his life as a human, that annoying time before he died and the Dark Lord elevated him to become something else, someone important with power and meaning to his existence. A meaning that had waned in the last few decades, but all he needed was a catastrophe with a massive death toll and he would have turned things around.

Surely Lucifer didn't blame him for his guild's inactivity? Not his fault Canadians were such bloody peacekeepers.

Before he could stomp around and grumble some more about his apartment, a portal opened, a mere rip that transcended space but not time. Nothing could turn back time, although he'd heard things could be sped up so that folks got the impression they'd projected into the future.

Hell's King himself stepped through, and Brody threw himself onto a knee. There was a time and place for disrespect, and it wasn't when the Devil bestirred himself for a rare visit.

"Rise, my loyal minion."

"Lord." Brody kept his head bowed. "You honor me with your presence."

"I do, don't I? What can I say? Best king evah!" Appearing as a man in his prime, Lucifer had thick hair black with hints of red, slightly tanned skin, a square jaw, and eyes with pupils of flame.

"How may I assist you, my lord?"

"Have you met the girl?"

"Do you speak of the woman across the hall?"

"Are you always this deliberately dumb?" Lucifer pinned him with a gaze.

"Just ensuring clarity, my king."

"Why do that? Do you know how many fights would be averted if people took the time to make sure they understood? It would be bad for business." The Devil grinned.

Rather than follow the twisted logic, he answered the first question. "I spoke to the female living across the way." He pointed.

"What did you think of her?"

"She's small." Short actually, not even reaching his chin. Hard to tell about her physique under her bulky sweater. She'd worn glasses around her neck and her hair in a sloppy tail atop her head.

"But she's got great birthing hips." Lucifer spread his hands.

"If you say so, sir."

"I do say so, loyal Brody. How long before you find someone to plant a seed in her belly?"

"As soon as possible."

"Make it quicker! We've no time to waste."

"Understood, but you do realize I arrived only a moment before you. I'll need to set up an office—"

"Excuses!" Lucifer slashed a hand through the air, and the building shook as thunder crashed.

"Necessities. My orders, which you wrote, indicated utmost secrecy about this endeavor."

"The quietest. Can't have He-Who-Keeps-Changing-His-Name hearing about it." Lucifer rolled his eyes.

"Meaning I must accomplish your task in an organized manner. Once I have a process in place, we'll bring over the demons who pass submissions."

"Not just demons. I've got plans to breed the humans with every species I can lay my hands on." The Devil rubbed them together.

"Any particular type of demon you'd like me to arrange for this Posie Ringwald?"

"Someone special. Not a dummy. He should be the commanding type. Smart, too. But loyal. I want her child to be something special."

That seemed rather specific and lengthy. Given Lucifer's interest, Brody had to wonder if the lord was finally going to step out on Mother Earth. That would cause some chaos if she ever found out. Maybe some deaths. Perhaps a return to Hell and his actual job… "Perhaps you have suggestions on who I should match her with."

"The whole point in starting up a matchmaking service was to free up my valuable time. I'm a busy man, you know. Contracts to sign. Souls to collect."

"I thought you had underlings doing that."

"Who do you think oversees them?"

"Isn't that the task for your other employees?" In many respects, Hell was a modern-day machine with many moving parts and Lucifer the linchpin that held it together.

"Are you implying I'm not needed?" the Dark Lord huffed, smoke curling from his nostrils.

"Never! Without your expertise, Hell would be in shambles. I merely asked for guidance because it is well known that none could ever aspire to be as grand a pimp as you." He'd seen the made-for-HellTV movies on the romances the devil engineered. *A Demon and his Witch, A Demon and his Psycho*, and his personal favorite, *Hell's Kitty*.

"I am the king of pimps. Although I'm not fond of wearing the chains." Lucifer brushed a hand down his red velour jacket, the buttons open-mouthed skulls with glowing eyes.

"I shall endeavor to do your bidding and prove myself worthy of your trust, oh mighty Dark Lord."

"You'd better. And don't use the word trust. You know I have issues with it." The Devil grimaced. "Do me a favor. While you're over here, toss a few bum-chica-wa-was into some you-know-whats," he said, poking his finger through a hole created by two more. He waggled his brows.

"Yes, sir." He lied. He'd been celibate for more than century now and saw no reason to break that chain.

Lucifer smiled. "This is going to be a most excellent endeavor."

No wonder they called him the king of lies.

One month later, Brody sat behind a desk with too much paperwork, the pile about to get higher since Karina, distracted by a pretty human, lost her demon target. It didn't help this failure would be compounded by a lack of pregnant humans and three possible abortions—meaning three soldiers, with pure souls, lost to Heaven.

The problems didn't end there. He'd already dispatched a team to handle the man in hospital with the bleeding groin, screaming about the date he'd gone on with the woman sporting teeth in her vagina. He'd be sending a scathing report back to the Guild in Hell about their screening process.

Brody missed the fires of Hell, and he probably wouldn't see them anytime soon given he'd yet to find Posie, his neighbor across the hall, the perfect match. Not for a lack of trying. The woman said no to everyone he shoved in her direction. He kind of admired that about her, even as he was determined to find her a match.

There had to be someone out there that could melt her Canadian pussy and spread those legs apart. And no matter how many naked dreams he had about the woman, it wouldn't be him.

6

MAYBE I SHOULD GET A CAT. Getting close to thirty-seven, single, and childless, led to Posie thinking about things she'd sworn she'd never do. Maybe she should become the woman who lived alone with felines. Who wore sweaters all the time and cotton briefs instead of bikini lace panties. She was already the crazy lady keeping tabs on her neighbor.

In her defense, he kept odd hours and even weirder company. Which was saying a lot considering the group living on the second floor.

She'd seen the guy across the hall more than a few times the month after he moved in, usually exiting his place, wearing that oversized cloak, his head hidden in the shadow of his hood. She'd yet to see his face and spent more time wondering than she should why he hid it.

She'd not spoken to him since that night she'd helped him with his stubborn key, nor had he required any more help. The next day a locksmith had come by and swapped the lock out for a keypad that beeped. If it weren't for the fact she'd taken to peeking every time she heard it going *blip, beep, bop* in the hall, she'd never see him.

She couldn't say as much for his guests. She couldn't seem to avoid them. They visited at all hours. Men. Women. Other. Which wasn't meant to be rude. Some of them had androgynous appearances that made it impossible to tell.

Many of his guests appeared to enjoy cosplay just like the downstairs neighbors. The man who appeared as a centaur was extremely well done. Too well done, given he'd ensured the ensemble kept the expression "hung like a horse" very true.

He tried to chat with her as if he weren't dressed as a mythical creature with a realistic prosthetic hanging out, but she'd huddled against the far side of the elevator, ignoring his smile. When those doors opened, she ran for her apartment, slammed that door shut, and locked it, even leaned on it for good measure. No surprise, horse-y man went to visit the guy across the hall.

Perhaps it was time to think of moving. That night, she searched the rental ads, suppressing a shiver when she heard a distant neigh. After hours of searching, she came to the conclusion this place still provided the best deal around.

It would have been tolerable if only his guests didn't appear to run into her on purpose. As she left her place in the morning, on a strict schedule to get to work, they'd exit his apartment in a hurry, smiles wide and brash with too many teeth. As they waited for the elevator, they always felt a need to chat.

"Hey, darling—"

"Where you been—"

"How about you and I—"

She never let them finish. "Not interested." Her only reply, and before they could engage her in conversation, she either locked herself back inside her apartment or left quickly for work.

But the overtures didn't stop. Every day this week she'd been practically accosted in the halls, forced to socialize. Bad enough she had to say hello to people all day long at work; she wasn't about to start at home.

And she had only one person to blame for it. Her mysterious neighbor across the hall.

It took her three more days before she got the nerve to knock on his door and do something about it. Three days because she practiced what she'd say, her favorite and least charitable one being, "*Excuse me, sir, but could you please ask yours guests to sew their mouths shut before I sew it for them?"*

She wanted to be nice. It killed her to be rude. However, she also wasn't about to continue living like this.

I am strong. Nothing to fear. He's just a man. Doesn't hurt to ask. The worst that will happen is he says no.

Or so she hoped as she mustered the gumption to knock on his door.

When the portal flung open, she almost flinched. A good thing she'd not remained standing close because he loomed in the opening. Big. Wide. And still wearing that stupid cloak even inside.

Did he have a problem with drafts? Perhaps she'd caught him about to go out.

"Can I assist you?" Spoken in that deep, low growl.

"I'm sorry to bother you." As a Canadian, she had to start with an apology, especially since she was about to be somewhat rude and demanding.

"Then why knock?"

"Excuse me?"

"You're apologizing for interrupting what I was doing, therefore making me wonder what could be so important that you felt a need to do so."

The convoluted twist had her blinking. "Would you prefer I wasn't sorry?"

"It would be more honest."

"I see. In that case then, I'm not sorry I knocked because I have something important to say."

"Doubtful."

This conversation wasn't going well at all, but she forged ahead anyhow. "I've come to ask if you could speak to your guests about respecting the privacy of those in the building. Especially in the elevator."

"Has there been an issue? Did someone accost you? They know they're not supposed to."

"I should hope not given it's against the law."

"Then what's the problem?" he snapped.

"They keep trying to talk to me."

"And?"

"I'd prefer they didn't."

"Let me get this straight. When you're in the common areas, and my guests run into you, they are to avoid speaking to you because you're antisocial?"

She almost winced because it sounded bad when he said it. Very un-Canadian. But she couldn't stop now. She forged ahead, taking the advice of her online virtual psychologist who told her she should confront her anxiety. "I'm glad you understand."

"Actually, I don't."

"I really would like it if you could help, as I suffer from anxiety."

He snorted. "The current trend. Everyone is anxious. Deal with it."

"I am, by asking you to speak to your guests."

"If you don't want to talk, then don't."

"But—"

"If we're done…" Not even a question as he moved to shut the door.

She rushed to say, "Could you also perhaps speak to them about wearing some kind of covering in public if they have certain areas exposed?" Her cheeks heated at her bold statement.

"Are you implying someone came into the building without their pants?" He sounded quite incredulous, his voice a low and rumbly timber. The velvety kind heard on the radio, but did he have the features to match?

"Only the one time. Your friend, the one dressed as a centaur."

His tone crept an octave higher. "You saw Frederick's horse ass?"

"I don't know his name, and it's not that his costume wasn't realistically detailed. It was just a little *too* detailed, if you understand what I mean."

"I do and I don't. Have any of my other guests appeared non-human to you?"

What an odd way of phrasing it. "If you mean have I seen elves and demons and other cosplay visitors, then the answer is yes. You're a popular guy."

"Not really. They're only showing because we're doing business."

The mention brought a frown. "What business?"

"I manage a matchmaking service."

Of all the answers… She blinked at him. "Excuse me, did you say you run a dating agency?"

"Yes."

She couldn't help it. She laughed. Hard and to the point that she almost wiped tears.

He crossed his arms—clad in black fabric—over his chest. His hands were, as usual, gloved. "I fail to understand your amusement."

She snorted. "Which is probably part of your problem. I have a hard time believing you're some kind of matchmaker given you look like the Grim Reaper."

"Thank you."

"That wasn't a compliment."

"You appear to be indicating my appearance is an issue." He glanced down. "I was assured these garments were suitable for this plane."

"Maybe if you were on a *Game of Thrones* set. Or some kind of movie where everyone dies and you steal their souls." Too late. She spoke and couldn't retract the words. He'd probably be peeved. She'd have to apologize.

Instead, the hood cocked to the side. His tone held a query. "What do you think I am dressed in?"

As if he didn't know. "A giant cloak for starters.

Gloves. And while I can't see what you're hiding under there, I am going to go out on a limb and assume it's just as black."

"You see my overgarments?" A surprised query.

"Kind of hard to miss."

"What about my face?"

"What about it? If you're asking if I could pick you out of a lineup, then the answer is no. Which you should know given you never seem to leave your apartment without hiding it."

"This is most fascinating." His gloved hands went to the hood, and he pulled it back. "Do you see me now?"

Goodness he was pretty. And she didn't think that often. Her neighbor had blond streaked, thick hair falling in slight waves, a very masculine face with a rugged jaw sporting a hint of a beard, and the most vivid and bright blue eyes, like sea ice in daylight.

"Well look at that, you have a face." Again, not the most brilliant reply.

His lips twitched. "I do. I just don't often show it."

"Which is your business. I didn't mean to trick you into revealing it."

"No. I'm glad we had this conversation. It was extremely enlightening."

"Again, really sorry to have bothered you. Best of luck with your dating operation." Which she might anonymously call in to make sure it was legit and not some front for some kinky sex club for people who liked to pretend they were mythical creatures.

Did that make him the dungeon master?

He'd probably look good in leather and chains.

7

BRODY LEANED against his door and pondered the revelation of his neighbor. She could see past the glamour that the demons and other species wore on the mortal plane. She saw him in his true form, wearing his uniform of office and not the meek façade that everyone else did. Every human, that was. His visitors perceived the truth beneath the spell veneer.

And so did Posie.

How was it possible? Her file, one of the few that had yet to move from the inbox to the out, indicated she was one hundred percent human. A human with a rare ability. It explained why the Dark Lord wanted her to mate with some of his soldiers. Being able to see beyond camouflaging magic would be a useful trait. However, it made his task more difficult. No wonder she'd rejected those he'd sent her way. She never saw the stunning good looks most of them wore. She thought they were playing dress up.

How could he make this work?

Tapping at her file, he barely paid any attention to the other robed figures moving around his apartment. They tended to pop in or out depending on their assignments, only wearing their cloaks when they were on a job and had to hide. The more time they spent on the mortal plane, the more his reapers tucked away the overgarment. Walking amongst the humans. Fitting in with the masses. Undetectable with their cloaks hidden.

Before the idea could fully form, brimstone scented the air, bringing a nostalgia for home until he remembered the guild didn't provide cold, stimulating showers or even chillier baths congealed with essential oils.

"How are things going?" The Dark Lord appeared, looking quite dapper in his hunting garb. Robin Hood style with green tights, a vest, and even a jaunty cap.

"Excellent, sir. Currently averaging three to five hookups a night. And we just confirmed three pregnancies." About time. He'd been seriously contemplating influencing some congressmen to pass some laws about contraception and abortion. He still might.

"Only three!" Smoke spilled from Lucifer's nostrils and curled like snakes, hissing in his direction.

"It's not easy countering the birth control methods the humans use. Not to mention, it's been only just over a month since we started. Most of the subjects we're following haven't indicated if their cycle has been disrupted yet. I imagine the number will jump within the next few weeks."

"It better improve! I am counting on you, Brody. The good news is now that you're finding my demons their perfect matches, even if at first they don't succeed, they will keep banging their meat into that one special bun, which will eventually result in little minions."

"Perfect matches, my lord?" Brody frowned. "We sought compatible coital partners, of which the majority moved on after the fornication was complete."

"What?" The Devil gaped at him. "What are you running, a whorehouse? Wham bam, thank you and back to Hell?"

"Isn't that what you ordered? Your mission statement indicated you wanted as many hybrid births as possible. That requires coitus. The coitus is happening."

"But what about the love?" Lucifer clutched his chest and bellowed, "Bambi! Where in the blazes are you?" The Devil reached into the air and, from a rip through space, yanked his daughter, wearing a robe, her hair in an upsweep, and an annoyed expression on her face.

"Do you mind? I was about to have a bath."

"What's this I hear about Grim Dating being all about the sex and not the connection?" The Devil sounded quite put out.

Bambi appeared confused.

And so was Brody for that matter. "Love, sir? Since when does love matter?"

"It's always mattered, but it's taken me millions of years to realize it. To finally figure out that the strongest and wiliest come from love matches. It is children born of those kinds of unions that will make my army unstoppable."

"Fuck me, did that Ursula put a spell on you again?" Bambi slapped her hand on the Devil's forehead.

Lucifer knocked it down and scowled. "I am not sick. Turns out, all this time my belief that love was a weakness, an evil thing to be avoided at all costs, was actually a ploy by Heaven to weaken me." He shook his fist at the ceiling. "I'm on to you, angelic bastards. I should have known it was a lie given they're incapable of loving anyone but themselves because love

61

isn't perfect. Love isn't clean. Or kind. Love of people, country, and religion is the greatest evil of all and the reason behind the vilest acts."

Bambi blinked long, dark lashes before drawling, "Love is a crock of shit."

"What she said." Brody jerked his thumb at her. "It doesn't exist. And those that think they're in love usually end up falling out of it eventually."

Only once had Brody succumbed. With the lovely Louisa, who acted as his mother's chambermaid. She claimed to love him. Certainly faked it well enough when she sighed beneath him. Turned out, she sighed like that for his mother and father, too. And the captain of the guard. And the cook. And... He learned his lesson. But not before Louisa's other lover, the captain of the guard, killed him.

Was it any wonder he volunteered to become a reaper? With just one caveat. He'd enjoyed dragging her soul and that of his murderer to Hell.

"Love is ever evolving, just like the universe. Why do you think Gaia and I keep coming together and then splitting apart?" Lucifer exclaimed.

"I thought it was because the make-up sex was so good," Bambi replied, sitting cross-legged on the floor since Brody still had almost no furniture. She appeared to be wearing something metallic under the robe. She glanced around. "Are you ever going to decorate?"

"I have all that I need." A desk with a chair. A mattress on the floor in the bedroom.

"Nonsense," Lucifer exclaimed. "I can't have the head of Grim Dating living in such poverty. It reflects badly on me. Not to mention, austerity is something my brother always condoned. You should know by now I'm more into indulgence." Lucifer snapped his fingers, and from the ether, a creature appeared, squat and bald with scaly green skin.

"Pokie," Bambi exclaimed. "Long time no see."

"My fair mistress." Pokie sketched a bow in her direction. "You are looking more covered than usual."

"You like?" She shrugged the robe off her shoulder. "I read an article detailing how less is sometimes more."

Lucifer agreed. "The author of that article was right. Nothing better than when Gaia dresses in her Victorian era clothes. So many layers to peel to get to the juicy center."

It gave Brody a sudden urge to find a Tootsie Roll lollipop, a strange treat given to him by a dryad who'd spent an inordinate amount of time sucking hers and asking him if he liked it.

"Brody, I'd like you to meet the best man servant a Dark King could ever have. Philokrates. He's the last of the Atlanteans. Brilliant people. Shame about what happened."

Everyone had heard of the tragedy. None spoke of it. It occurred during one of Lucifer and Gaia's breakups.

"Sir." Brody inclined his head.

Philokrates snorted. "Not a sir, Commander." He looked to the king. "You bellowed?"

"I did. I need your interior design skills to transform this dreary apartment into a proper boudoir." Lucifer swept a hand.

"You thinking red velvet and gold tassels?" Bambi asked, an appraising eye taking in the space.

"Or do we want to go chrome, shag, and leather?" Lucifer mused, rubbing the goatee on his chin.

"How about we keep it looking like an office since none of the actual hookups happen here?" Brody interjected.

"Actually, boy, that's about to change. The operation is about to expand. I'm adding the British Reaper Guild, as well as the Netherlands. We are going international, people."

"We are?" Bambi appeared just as surprised.

"Yes, which means you need to get your ass back to Hell, daughter, and keep on top of things. We'll need to triple the application process. I want more babies!"

"And you will get those babies. I will ride my team as hard as I did that football team in ninety-three," she swore. And then she was gone, a lingering scent of perfume and brimstone the only sign left behind.

"Ah, she does me proud. Just don't tell her. I'd hate to kill her for getting cocky." Lucifer crooked his finger. "Let's go."

"I don't really have the time—"

"It wasn't a request."

Brody found himself yanked close. The Devil never traveled by mundane means. He snapped his fingers, and they were standing in a massive office with windows overlooking the city. So many windows... The opposite of the guild in Hell.

"What is this place?"

"Your new office."

"Mine?" His eyes widened as he took another glance.

A massive desk of polished wood took up the most space, behind it a leather chair so plush it cradled his body when the Devil shoved him into it and spun it around.

"Tada! Welcome to Grim Dating headquarters. Nice, eh?" The Devil winked.

"Seems rather lavish." But he couldn't help admiring it. The bigger guilds in Hell had luxuries his could only dream of.

"It is the height of decadence. And necessary. Think big, boy. This operation is about to get huge."

"I thought the plan was to remain low-key?"

"Fuck hiding what we're doing." Lucifer slammed a fist into his palm, and thunder boomed outside. "It might do those bastards in Heaven some good to get nervous. Maybe they'll react and give me a hint at what's happening behind those pearly gates."

"You think a war is coming?"

"Let's just say you should keep your scythe sharp. But enough about the possible futures I am trying to manipulate." The Devil fixed him with a flame-lit stare. "According to my reports, you've yet to find someone special for Posie Ringwald. I'm disappointed, Brody."

That wasn't something anyone, even a reaper, wanted to hear the Devil say. "I've been trying, sir."

"Not hard enough!"

"She sees through glamour," he blurted out, hating to give an excuse, but an angry Devil was one that needed placating.

Lucifer smiled. "I know all about her ability to see past the facade. A rare gift, which is why it's important you pair her with the right fellow."

"Which is the problem. I've been trying." To the point she complained at his door the previous night, looking nervous at first and then feisty. He shrugged. "She sees everyone I send as they are. She thinks they're dressing up and is rejecting all I send her way without hesitation."

"Because you're sending her the wrong kind of guys. She needs someone human looking. Someone who will fool her senses."

Brody grimaced. "That doesn't leave us with many options. Almost every single demon is out, leaving werewolves in between full moons, vampires, wizards, the fallen." He ticked off his fingers. "Who else?"

"You forgot the most obvious of all."

"Who?" he asked.

The Devil smiled. "Reapers."

"Set her up with one of my crew?" He frowned, and yet he shouldn't have. A few of his people had been playing with some of the human potentials. In the case of Gary, he'd moved in with his mortal lady friend.

"I don't care which reaper bangs her. You, someone else. Doesn't matter so long as someone is getting into her pants and soon."

He glanced around the new office and realized something that might impede the Dark Lord's wishes. "You do realize if I move my operation to this office, then I won't have the same opportunities to have her run into potentials at the apartment building."

"You could sign her up to become a member of Grim Dating. Humans love free things."

"She'll say no." He knew that for a certainty.

"Yes, she is rather stubborn like that." The Devil rubbed his chin. "Don't worry. I have a plan."

More ominous words were never spoken.

8

"You're fired."

"What? I don't understand." Posie stood in front of her boss's desk.

Mr. Kulley—in his late fifties, balding, with a paunch—was usually a very affable and kind man. Even now he looked apologetic, but firm on his stance. "I am sorry, Posie, but I'm afraid the new Mrs. Kulley isn't comfortable with you being my secretary anymore." The new Mrs. Kulley being a young thing who thought everyone was eyeballing her man. Apparently, she could use glasses.

"I've worked for you for eight years."

"I know. I am so very, very sorry. I promise to give you an excellent reference and three months' severance."

"This isn't fair." Her voice rose in pitch.

"Six months."

No amount of pleading changed his mind. She was still numb with the news when she got to her building. She grabbed her mail as if on autopilot, barely paying attention to the green lady who walked in, her bits covered by leaves, alongside the guy with the long beard. The D&D wizard player. He waved. By reflex, she waved back.

Given she was stuck staring into space for a moment, she missed the elevator and had to wait for it to come back down. When the door opened, a looming shadow filled it for a moment, and then the hood came down and her neighbor from across the hall peered at her.

"Are you okay, Posie?" he asked, brow creased in concern.

"How do you know my name?" Because they'd never actually been introduced.

He pointed to the mail in her hand.

"Oh." She waited for him to exit the cab, except he didn't move.

"You didn't answer my question. Why do you appear upset?"

"I got fired today." Since he didn't seem keen on getting out, she entered the cab with him and pressed the button for their floor. He still made no move, and the doors slid shut.

"Why were you fired?"

"Because a mistress-turned-wife said Mr. Kulley had to get rid of me." Her lips turned down. "As if I'd have ever flirted with Mr. Kulley. He's older than my father."

Her neighbor jerked as if shoved, and she squinted at the space beside him. It shimmered, as if hot. "That's terrible," he said. "But also fortuitous."

"How is that lucky?" she snapped. "I have no job."

"It so happens I am in need of a secretary."

"First off, what makes you think I'd be good for that job? Is it because I'm a woman?"

"No, but because you are a secretary. Or were."

"Says who?"

"I saw you. Office on Huegl Street with a window overlooking the sidewalk."

A valid reply for his reasoning. Still...

He spoke quicker as the elevator slowed. "I need a secretary to handle my affairs. You need a job. Seems like the perfect match." For some reason he winced and glared at the heat spot beside him.

She'd seen what kind of business he ran. Out of his apartment. No way was she taking part in that. "Thank you for offer; however, I'm going to have to decline."

"Why?"

"For one, I don't believe you really run a dating service. Look at you." She swept a hand. "Your outfit is more suitable for a funeral. Your expression as well. Would it kill you to smile?"

"Not me, but I can't speak for those that might see it."

"See what I mean about your sense of humor? And you expect me to believe you run a successful business?"

"What does my expression and ability to jest have to do with matching people up?" He followed her onto their floor once the doors slid open.

"Everything. People who use matchmakers need to trust them. And I'll be honest, you don't look the type to care if people get their happily ever after."

"Not you, too," he grumbled. "What does love and happiness have to do with it?"

Her brows arched. "Everything."

"My instructions were to pair humans and...er... other people together."

"Instructions from who?"

Again, it was if he meant to say one thing but settled for something else. "My boss."

"And why does your boss want people to get together?"

"In order to increase the population, of course."

That brought a frown. "Hold on, that doesn't sound like dating, more like a baby-making scam."

"You misunderstand. I'm looking to ensure the

people who meet form a bond for a lifetime, which usually includes a family."

"Why does it sound like you're reciting something you've heard but don't believe in?"

"The truth? I have a hard time believing in this whole love thing. Love is a messy, painful thing."

"On that we agree." Posie had tried it a few times. It never worked out. And as time ticked on, and her paranoia increased, she stopped even trying.

"This matchmaking thing... It wasn't my idea, but I'm kind of stuck with it. And I could use help." He almost sounded sincere.

"I am not working across the hall."

"What if I said I now have an actual office?"

"That isn't in your living room or bedroom?"

His lips twitched. "As of today, I have an entire building at my disposal."

If true, that did more or less legitimize it. "What's the salary?"

He mentioned something twice what she was making now, with benefits and a pension plan, plus a month vacation per year. It seemed too good to be true, but she couldn't exactly be picky. She held out her hand. "Very well. I accept your terms, Mr...?"

"Reaper. Brody Reaper. Welcome to Grim Dating, Posie Ringwald."

The leather grip was warmer than expected and brief. He yanked his hand away as if burned.

"When do I start?" she asked.

"Tomorrow."

For her first day, Mr. Reaper—the fakest name she'd ever heard—told her to present herself at HR, second floor, in a building at the heart of downtown. Not a bad commute. A single subway each way.

The building itself proved more impressive than expected. Three stories, with a massive sign out front, gunmetal and etched in black letters: Grim Dating.

And it appeared their shtick was that the employees wore robes. The moment she entered, she saw one, sitting behind the desk, hood down low, body hunched as they played on a phone. As she stepped into the building, the robed figure sprang to action and swung a scythe that stopped an inch from her nose.

"Ha! So close. Almost got you," a male voice exclaimed.

"You're lucky I don't have a weak bladder," was her retort. "I hope you don't greet customers like this."

The guy in the reaper robe propped his scythe and freed his head from his hood. "You saw that?"

"Kind of hard to miss. Is this an act for the job?"

"Er. No. Um. I have to go." The guy practically ran with his giant farmer's knife.

There wasn't much to see. The now empty desk, a few conference rooms, also currently empty, their glass windows allowing a clear view inside.

At the far end, a bank of elevators. Mr. Reaper had said second floor for HR. The elevator opened immediately, and in under a minute, she was on the second floor with the many doors.

Marketing. Research. Human Guises. Animal Guises.

She really didn't want to see in there. She hurried to the far end to the one marked HR, the sign taped over the previous one that said Supply Closet.

She didn't hold high hopes when she knocked on the door.

It opened, and a small face peered at her, blinking owlishly behind glasses. "Who are you?"

"Posie Ringwald. I was hired by Mr. Reaper to be his secretary."

"Aren't you an interesting choice." The woman eyed her up and down, her pupils enlarging to the point of overtaking the lens then suddenly shrinking to size as she quipped, "Won't you come inside so we can handle the paperwork."

Inside was as small as expected. The lower shelves had been removed to allow for a chair and a table to act as a desk. A stool perched in front of it. The only other thing was a laptop with a flame symbol lit on the back of it. She'd never seen the brand before.

"Choose a seat. Make yourself comfortable."

Posie eyed the three-legged stool and wondered when it had been last tested. She hoped she didn't land on her ass as she sat.

It held.

"Welcome, Posie Ringwald, to Grim Dating, a Hell World subsidiary. As you can see, we are an up-and-coming, successful company."

She glanced at the generic giant bottles of cleaning solution overhead and couldn't help the sarcasm. "Obviously making a killing."

"Not anymore. Now instead of taking people's lives, we're ruining them because everyone knows marriage is a crock." Said with a wide smile.

"If you don' believe in Grim Dating, then why work here?"

"Excuse me?"

"Well, you just said you're ruining people's lives."

Her mouth dropped open. "You heard that?"

"You said it quite clearly."

The woman blinked. "Excuse me a minute while I go freak out."

"Why freak out?"

"Eep." The woman fled, and Posie frowned.

Now what? Had she sat down in the wrong office? Or was someone playing a prank?

She stood, but before she could exit the closet, suddenly he was there, a massive shadow over the door, broad, tall, looming, and ominous.

She scowled. "Come to laugh at your joke?"

"You're early. I meant to arrive before you and warn Mrs. Lenore."

"Warn her about what?"

"You." He tugged the hood, showing off a quirky smile. "See, I don't really have an HR department yet. I'm afraid the pressure of pretending got to Mrs. Lenore."

"You could have just told me the truth."

He winced. "Apparently, I won't have a choice."

"Is the job fake, too?"

He shook his head. "No. It's quite real, I assure you. And could get as interesting as your meeting with Mrs. Lenore. You might have surmised by now we don't exactly deal in regular human types."

"They're still human even if they dress up."

Once more he grimaced. "I wouldn't recommend saying that to them. Some can be quite touchy."

"I'll keep that in mind. So where is my office?" Hopefully he didn't give her a bathroom stall or a stairwell.

They went to the third floor, a massive space. In the center of the room was a circular reception desk with a woman sitting primly. Her hair coiled atop her head looked like real snakes.

Mr. Reaper waved a hand in her direction. "This is our security for this floor. Medusa, say hello to my new secretary, Posie Ringwald."

A silver gaze, almost mirror-like, lifted to meet hers. "You're rather red-blooded for this level. Are you sure that's a good idea?" she asked her boss.

Mr. Reaper leaned close. "Be good and remember Ms. Ringwald is going to be my eyes in this place. She sees more than the average person."

Say what? Posie almost frowned. Yes, a compliment, but a strange one.

"This isn't wise," Medusa hissed, and her snake wig shook with her.

"Take it up with the big boss."

Medusa's lips drew back. "Hail—" She paused and slewed a silvery gaze at Posie. "Hail to the chief."

Weird. Reaper moved away, and Posie followed as he gave her a quick rundown." "This level has all the upper management for Grim Dating, my lieutenants, whom you'll meet as they come into the office."

"How many people work for you?"

"It's a fluid number, but any given day? Close to sixty. And then there are the potentials."

Her nose wrinkled. "That's an odd way of referring to them."

"What else would you suggest?" he asked as they

walked past doors framed by frosted windows. No peeking inside on this level.

"Clients."

"Rather impersonal."

"So are 'potentials.'"

"Our focus group on level two said it tested more positive."

"Wait, you have a focus group?"

"Since week two."

"How long have you been in business?"

"Almost five weeks."

"So since the night you moved in, basically?"

"The very next day."

His step slowed at the far end before a wall of frosted glass with a door. It opened at his approach. She entered a lavish space, carpeted, with two couches and a fat chair around a low window inlaid with a mosaic. Bleached wood paneling. A skylight that streamed daylight and a desk so sleek and clean she wanted to stroke it.

"You have a really nice office." She wondered where he'd hide her. Maybe in another closet.

"This isn't my office. This is where you'll be working. You will handle people arriving for appointments with me."

She gaped at the space that was five times the size of her last reception post. Not only did she have a big desk and windows, she had her own kitchenette, bathroom, and even a couch, with a television for when she took her break. In many respects, it was nicer than her apartment.

"This is my office?" He swung open a pair of doors at the far end, and she found his space was even bigger and more lavish.

Five minutes later, she sat at her new workstation, staring at the screen for her laptop, which showed Mr. Reaper's schedule as clear until eleven. Surely, she should be doing something? The place was immaculate. The phone on the desk never rang. No papers required filing.

The only thing she had to deal with was curious faces. They kept popping in without her noticing. Empty room one second and the next, *poof*, someone in a robe was standing there.

The first time she squeaked, they squeaked, and Reaper came bolting out.

He took one look at her and the person who snuck in before grumbling, "Sending a memo now."

A memo about what? She had two more unexpected visitors pop in then finally her first real job of the day.

Murray Franklin entered, his hoofs well done, the pants had a really good hind leg shape to them. The horns could have been a bit longer though, given the satyr look he was obviously going for.

Upon seeing her, he leered and grabbed his crotch.

"Do that again and I'll have you arrested for behaving indecently." Posie wasn't about to let anyone think that working at a dating agency made her receptive to any kind of gross behavior.

"Don't be like that, baby. You know you want this." He gyrated his hips.

"Not one bit." To soften the blow, she added, "I'm sure one day you'll find someone who thinks your *tiny* horns"—she stressed—"are adorable."

"Little?" He uttered a bleat and slapped his hands over his forehead.

"If you'll have a seat, I'll see if Mr. Reaper is available."

The afternoon didn't get any less strange. A virtual parade of cosplaying people went by her desk that day and the next. Some less into the cosplay than others. One guy was actually rather handsome, if you ignored the fact he wore actual metal armor.

He clanged quite a bit and wasn't impressed when she said, "Do you need to oil the joints often?"

She finished her first week and had to admit, while it started out slow, it did prove interesting. If hard to comprehend. Mr. Reaper didn't really need her, but if he wanted that prestige and to pay her, she wouldn't say no.

She actually enjoyed it and did get a spurt of

pleasure out of making the security guard flinch every morning when she uttered a bright and cheery, "Good Morning, Barry. Your scythe is looking mighty shiny today."

9

THE DEVIL'S PLAN WORKED. Brody managed to hire Posie, giving him all the opportunities needed to throw potential matches at her. The problem being, he had no idea who to start with. She'd shown no interest in any of his appointments thus far.

He tended to have talks with first-timers to make sure they understood the rules. He flashed his scythe for good measure to make sure they understood the consequences if they fucked up.

Not one of his clients got a second look or flirty smile from her. A few got verbally schooled. Posie might have that innate Canadian kindness that made her apologize all the time, but that didn't stop her from putting people in their place.

"Excuse me, Gallops All Night, but this location requires you wear pants. In your case, as you're giving

horses a bad name, you really shouldn't be ignoring that rule."

She had a level of efficiency that didn't go unnoticed. The Devil showed up after her first week on the job.

"She is good at handling those fuckers," Lucifer noted, having turned the wall in his office into a one-way mirror.

"Only because she still thinks they're costumes." Which he didn't understand at first. How could anyone be that oblivious? Then he used the internet he'd heard so much about. Once he saw examples of cosplay, he understood her doubt.

Which made him wonder, if she didn't believe, then were they wasting their time with veneers of magic over their true natures? Perhaps the humans would be like Posie and think it was all fake.

For his part, Brody had stopped wearing his hood around her. No point. She'd accuse him of looking like Death again. She had no idea how accurate that was.

With her not showing interest in any of the current potentials, that left reapers. Lucifer wanted her with someone of a higher echelon than simple peon. That sounded like his lieutenants. He went through the list of his most trusted reapers. Joel. Barry. Julio. Maurice.

All good men. But were they right for Posie? The

Dark Lord being extremely interested in her case meant he couldn't get this wrong.

Perhaps if he got to know her a little better, more than what her file contained, he'd have a better feel for her needs. Which might be why he was knocking on her door at nine o'clock at night almost two weeks after she started working for him.

She didn't answer. Was she home? She had to be. He always knew when she left. Couldn't seem to help himself. Her soul called out to him.

Even now he could sense her on the other side of the door. Did she watch him? He pressed his eye to the peephole and heard her squeak.

"I know you're there." He always knew when she was near. Felt her in a way he didn't feel anyone else. "You can stop pretending."

"You do realize it's kind of late."

"Late? It's nine o'clock."

"Exactly," was her pert reply. "I'm in my pajamas."

"And?"

"A woman doesn't simply open the door to strangers in her night clothes."

"But we're hardly strangers."

"No, you're my new boss, which means"—she yanked open the door—"we should set some boundaries. Starting with, once I leave the office, I'm done work for the day. So whatever it is you need will have to wait until tomorrow. At the office."

He blinked. "Did you just tell me fuck off and not knock on your door?"

"Yes. But politely."

"What else?"

"Any other concerns I have can be dealt with at the office. Tomorrow." She went to close the door.

He couldn't help it. This constant failure to understand her grated. "Why are you so...so..." He struggled for a word.

"Bitchy?"

"I would have said standoffish," he lied. The Devil surely smiled.

"I don't see the point in getting close to people."

"Why?" This seemed contrary to most humans he encountered. His observation showed they preferred to surround themselves with souls. Even the useless ones.

She shrugged. "I prefer the quiet."

Living in a guild for a few centuries, he'd not realized how enjoyable quiet could be until his apartment emptied of people coming and going. At the same time, the lack of noise deafened him when he sat on his couch—a comfortable thing of dark gray fabric with red and orange cushions. The colors drawing out the pattern in the rug. After Lucifer had shown him his new office, and sprung the secretary surprise, he'd returned to find it fully furnished.

Thankfully not in the pink vomit Bambi covered the guild in.

When he returned, he'd have to order lots of dark paint.

If he returned. If he failed with Posie, the Dark Lord might not want him back.

He'd not learned much about her other than she was extremely antisocial, even more than him, and liked the quiet. Did that include during sex?

The thought took him so hard aback, he didn't react in time, and the door gently shut in his face. With the coup de grace being the click of the dead-bolt. Also known as the throwing down of the gauntlet.

"It is on, my prickly flower." He would find her not just a compatible sexual partner but a love match.

DESPITE HER ADMONITION to her new boss, the next morning when Posie opened her door to head out for work, he stood in the hall as if waiting for her.

"Morning, Mr. Reaper." She kept the greeting brisk as she locked her door and tugged the handle for good measure.

She'd learned awhile ago that if she didn't then she'd wonder if she'd actually locked it or closed it securely. It would weigh on her mind, making her almost sick with anxiety to the point she'd have to rush home early to check. Each time, her door was fine.

As she turned back—because she couldn't stare at her portal forever—she couldn't miss the fact he wore the cloak, the fluid black fabric currently thrown over his shoulders, meaning she saw his actual form in its entirety. Wide as she expected, no sign of a paunch, his slim-fitting button-up shirt tucked into slacks. A casual yet clean look not marred at all by the combat boots that she'd wager were steel-toe. The belt and his buckle were the same black as the rest of his ensemble. Yes, all black. What a surprise. There was a surprising number of staff who dressed just as darkly. Such a somber impression for what should be a mood-elevating business.

The very grim nature might be why she purposely did the opposite when she chose her own outfit for the day: a flowered bohemian-style skirt that flowed to her ankles, brown leather boots, a peasant style blouse in white, adorned with loops of chunky strung beads in every color. Over it, she wore a distressed jean jacket, and she carried a giant pink satchel.

His brows rose. "Did I miss a memo on rainbow day?"

"Did you forget about me saying no work until we're at the office?" Her tone was sweet but firm.

"I wasn't talking to you about work. Just being neighborly. It is, after all, the Canadian way."

She side-eyed him as they waited for the elevator. Had he meant that as a dig? In her defense, he did rouse her more feisty side. She had her reasons for pushing him away. Yet, like a bad perm that you tried to straighten, he kept coming back. "You're not Canadian, though."

"What can I say? You are contagious."

They entered the empty elevator cab, and their fingers bumped as they went to hit G for the ground floor. He wore gloves. Again. It made her wonder if he ever took them off. Did they hide something? Scars, perhaps?

As she exited the building, the heavy clouds in the sky drew her attention. Rain for sure. Hopefully not before she managed to get to the underground and the subway that would take her downtown to her new office.

A sleek car sat at the curb, black all over, shiny with tinted windows. Given the building they lived in, she was kind of surprised when a guy wearing a chauffeur's uniform—in a shade of slate—popped out and opened the door, gesturing with a hand. "Ma'am."

"I'm sorry. That's not for me." She began to walk away, only to hear Mr. Reaper clearing his throat.

"The car is mine. And as you can see, there's plenty of room for us both to ride to work."

"I don't need a ride." She clutched her bag to her chest. "Remember what I said about separation."

"This is just practicality. We're both going in the same direction. Already wasting carbon. Or do you enjoy denying a needy person a seat on the subway?"

She sucked in her lower lip. He did have a point. Still…that would put her awfully close to him.

"What if," he said, waving his driver off and standing by the open door, "I promise not to talk about work?"

If he didn't use the business as a topic, what did that leave? Could they travel in pure silence?

Her lips opened to say no, only to halt as a cold drop of water landed on the tip of her nose. A glance upward at the heavy clouds and another drop made it clear she wouldn't make it underground before the heavens let loose. Get wet or tolerate the boss in comfort?

She was being stupid. "I accept your offer but must insist on sharing the cost of gas."

He snorted. "Of course you will."

She sat on the farthest end of the seat, knees together, hands on her lap, while he lounged on his side, blending in with the dark interior as if wreathed in smoky shadows. The rain dumped in hard, fat pellets the moment the car pulled from the curb. She'd made the right decision. Perhaps he'd work while they travelled. She could read the book she'd started.

"Do you have any pets?"

She hadn't pulled her phone out quick enough. "No."

"Why not? Are you allergic?"

"Are you?" she countered.

"I don't actually know." He frowned.

"How do you not know?" she couldn't help but exclaim.

"I'm not usually on the same plane as animals."

"Planes aren't the only time you run into them." She rolled her eyes. "And on planes they're usually in cages. It's part of the aviation rules I think."

His lips quirked. "You misunderstand. I meant to say…" He paused. "I've led a sheltered existence and haven't really had a chance to encounter any animals in close quarters, although my glimpses while in public outdoor locations haven't led to any issues."

Mr. Reaper was a seriously strange guy at times. She wanted to ask why he'd led a sheltered existence, but then he might misconstrue that as interest. The wrong kind of interest.

"Best way to find out is visit a pet store. If your nose starts twitching when you enter, then chances are you're allergic."

"I might try that. I hear the felines in this world hunt the rats instead of conspiring with them." At her wide gaze, he grinned. "A jest."

"Are you always in character?" She had to ask because she'd noticed that some people took their outfits seriously. They even spoke differently, saying the most outrageous things at times, such as how their building was much better than the old guild, with its soot-covered stone.

"I don't think I understand the question."

"Forget it. It's probably rude to ask." She waved a hand and looked away, embarrassed.

"You still believe I'm playing at death."

"Aren't you?" She arched a brow.

"I never play."

"Did you change your name to Reaper, or were you actually born with it?"

"Depends on your definition of born. Are we talking physical birth or the one that comes after death?"

"There you go again. Talking as if you're really the Grim Reaper. Do you keep your scythe in the trunk?" She shouldn't tease, but he kept asking for it.

"Would you like to see it?"

Given she'd been sassing him? "No, I don't want to see your toy. What I'd like is to ride quietly to work. Maybe catch up on the news." She waggled her phone.

"You're difficult to decipher."

"It's not your job to figure me out. I'm not one of your clients."

He leaned forward. "Would you like to be?"

"No!" she exclaimed, perhaps a tad too vehemently. "I don't believe in artificial relationships." And then there was that whole birthday thing coming. She'd already sworn to herself she wouldn't commit to anything until she turned thirty-seven. Not long now… The question being, would she live to thirty-eight?

"So no matchmaking, but you are available?"

"Not interested. My life is just fine the way it is," she lied. It was boring and safe. And it would stay that way for the next few weeks. Then— She had to drag her mind away from that topic or she'd unravel it like a thread on a sweater. "If you're so good at matchmaking, how come you're single?"

"Who says I am?" He had a rakish smile.

"So you *are* dating someone?"

His smirk disappeared. "No. Nor do I have any intention of starting."

"Again, you don't see the irony of you being in charge of people's happiness when you're not into the idea yourself?"

"Touché, Ms. Ringwald. May I call you Posie?"

"No."

The car slid to a stop, and just as smoothly, he was out of the vehicle. He held out a gloved hand to assist her. She could have ignored it, but her Canadian kicked in and she grabbed hold, muttering a low, "Thanks."

"I'd say it was my pleasure, but you'd probably take offense." He steadied her on the pavement.

"Did you just insult me?"

"Yes, but I did it politely. See, I am catching on." He winked before he turned and strode away, not bothering to wait for her.

She held her head high and pretended she wasn't annoyed. She should be pleased he'd finally decided to leave her alone. Instead, she glowered. Especially given, even at this early hour, there were cosplayers out in full force. One that reminded her of a giant Groot but muddier. She wondered if he was the reason for more of those tree-dressing ladies who looked less like dryads and more like pinup girls for the Jolly Green Giant.

By the looks of it they were straggling in from the mixer held the night before—the Spring Fling, despite it being November. It wouldn't be the first time disheveled clients wandered in after a night of partying. They entered the building, but she never saw them leave. She didn't know why or what happened with them. Perhaps they took off the costumes and donned the dark robes.

All the employees of Grim Dating wore a robe like the boss, some flung over their shoulders, others —the freakiest ones—fully shrouded. She'd gotten used to seeing them practically drift around. They had a way of moving as if they floated. Disturbing but obviously some kind of illusion trick because of the cloak.

In the beginning, she might have thought they

took the whole Grim Dating theme too far; however, given their obvious success, perhaps they were on to something.

As she arrived at the top floor, she found a box on her desk and Brody—Mr. Reaper—standing over it, frowning at the contents.

"I don't know if I like it." He whirled and held out a business card. "What do you think?"

He wanted her opinion? She took the card from him and arched a brow at the cartoon reaper etched on it, the scythe digging into a heart beside the company title and website.

"It's—" She paused and thought of the clientele he served. The cosplayers who, according to internet research, lived their lives as the characters they dressed as. People who probably didn't have an easy time finding love. "I think it's actually perfect."

"You do?" He sounded most surprised.

"It's cute without being too cute. It gets across the point that you're open to things that other dating services might not be."

"I guess." He didn't sound convinced.

"If you don't like it, then tell your designer you want something new."

"I can't. Head office had these made." He scowled. "But I am drawing the line at the T-shirts."

"What T-shirts?" It was only as she spoke that she

saw the other box sitting on her chair, open, with fabric spilling out.

"What's wrong with them?"

"He's just complaining to hear his voice," announced Julio as he strode in.

"Fuck you," Reaper growled.

"No, thanks. You know I'm a ladies' man." Julio winked. He was a handsome man with tanned skin and dark hair. The epitome of sexy Latino. But not her type. She preferred her men tall, dark, and brooding. Kind of like her boss.

Oops. She wasn't supposed to think about him like that.

"What do you want?" Reaper scowled.

"I wanted to say keep the mugs! These are made for caffeine junkies." Julio—his cloak flung over his shoulder almost like a scarf—held up a massive cup. He wore a gray, form-fitting T-shirt and black jeans.

"They sent mugs, too? Show me." Brody, because he just didn't look like a Mr. Reaper with that expression, snatched it from Julio's hands and turned it around in his hands.

Julio began to extoll the virtues of it. The man had a silvered tongue. "Solid construction. Dishwasher safe. And the size is most excellent."

"It will take an entire coffee pot to fill," Posie remarked.

"You're right." Brody peered inside. "These we can use. But the T-shirts have to go."

"I'll have the boxes put in the dumpster," Julio declared.

"Throw them out? Why would you do that when you can use them for free marketing?" Posie exclaimed.

The men turned to look at her, but it was Brody who said, "Explain."

"Explain what? That it's a waste to throw out perfectly good merchandise?" She snatched one from the box and shook it out, the black T-shirt super cute with the Grim Reaper logo on the front. "People will wear these."

"Not me," Julio declared.

"Or me," said her boss.

"You're not who the marketing is for. You want people talking about Grim Dating. Free swag that they can wear is the best kind of advertising."

Brody rubbed his chin. "That might be useful for bringing in more of the humans. We're running into a shortage. But at the same time, it will make our actions more visible."

"Visibility is a supposed to be a good thing," she argued.

"Not if the wrong sorts get involved," Brody muttered. "Maybe we shouldn't get too loud."

The very idea that any company would want to

hide their success boggled the mind, but then again, perhaps he worried too much attention on a cosplayer dating service would draw negative reports and shaming on social media.

"Let me ask, what is your goal here?" Posie questioned.

"Making matches."

"These will help you do that by exposing your brand to a wider audience."

Brody's phone rang, screaming something about great big balls of fire. Her boss sighed. "What does he fucking want now?"

He answered, and she couldn't hear what was said other than Brody's clipped, "Yes, sir. Understood." He hung up. "Julio, we are going to take Ms. Ringwald's suggestion and distribute those shirts. Figure out the best locations to reach viable potentials. The boss says we will have ten thousand more by evening."

"Ten thousand?" she said faintly. The cost boggled the mind, not to mention, the timing of the call and the instructions. Almost as if... She eyed her office suspiciously. Was she being watched?

"The owner doesn't like to do things small," Brody said, distracting her.

"I will handle it at once, Commander." Julio saluted, and as he swept past her to grab the box, his cloak swirled, a splendid affair that made the fabric seem even more fluid than smoke.

She wondered if the other employees thought it odd that she chose to not wear one. Then again, her employer never asked her to. Probably because he knew she'd say no.

Once they were alone, Brody rubbed his hands together. "That was an excellent suggestion. Got any more ideas?"

"Me?"

"Yes, you." Brody beamed at her, and she couldn't help but actually smile back. Mr. Kulley hadn't been one to care about her opinion.

"I've only just started working here. I barely understand how things work yet." She'd spent her entire time thus far just handling Brody's appointments. No filing. No typing. She didn't even have to answer a phone. The appointments were set up elsewhere and appeared on her computer. She'd never done less in her life, and she kind of felt guilty he was overpaying her.

"Well, if you think of a way I can improve business, let me know."

"Don't you have a marketing department?"

He scowled. "Thus far their ideas haven't been useful. These modern times aren't what they're used to."

She blinked. "Are you saying they don't know

how to use social media to leverage your business?"
The very idea shocked.

"See what I mean? You obviously have a good
grasp of what's needed to take the business to the
next level. Perhaps we can discuss it over lunch.
Which," he said, raising a finger to forestall her argument, "is work. Not pleasure."

"I shouldn't leave my post."

His grin proved teasing as he said, "Then order in
a meal. We'll eat in my office."

It sounded reasonable. So why was she nervous
as the noon hour approached? Not wanting to over-
step any bounds, she had a proper lunch delivered—
thick sandwiches, drinks, and chips. Not exactly
gourmet, but not completely fast food either.

At noon on the dot, she knocked at his door. It
swung open immediately, startling her.

Brody beamed. "On time. I do like that about you,
Ms. Ringwald."

"I'm a person who likes punctuality."

"In my profession it's also quite important," he
admitted.

Which made no sense. How did being on time
help him match people?

"Lunch is here."

"Excellent."

He snatched the bag from her hand and strode to
his desk, where he laid it out. Then he sat behind the

massive piece of furniture, sandwich in hand, eating it over the wrapper, a napkin nearby. For all that he dressed like Death, he had impeccably clean manners.

"Tell me, Ms. Ringwald, have you arrived at any ideas as to how we can recruit more potentials?"

"How about we start by not calling it recruiting?" she quipped.

Most people would have laughed. He nodded. "A valid point. I shall endeavor to watch my language."

"Have you thought of having a booth at the comic-cons that pop up in various cities?"

"The what?"

She spent a few minutes explaining. Then a few more minutes behind his desk pulling up websites and images. By the time they'd finished lunch over an hour later, they'd progressed from Mr. and Ms. to first names.

Why, she was almost at ease around him until he said, "I need to step out this afternoon, but I shall return in time to provide you a lift for your journey home."

"No need. I'll be perfectly fine." She cleared the remains of their lunch from his desk.

"It's still raining," he pointed out.

"I need a new umbrella, so I'll just buy one on my way home."

"There is such a thing as being too stubborn," he chided.

"Actually, it's more about being polite. You shouldn't have to go out of your way to come back here to give me a ride. You don't owe me one, and I shouldn't expect one. So go to your meeting and don't worry about me. I'll make my own way home." Before he could argue further, she swept out of his office and returned to her desk.

She waited for him to leave, only the door to his office never opened. Odder still, when she knocked to deliver a rare stack of folders, he didn't reply. When she popped her head around the door, it was to find him nowhere to be seen. He'd somehow managed to escape without her notice.

With him gone, and no appointments to manage, she expected to finish reading her book, and yet around midafternoon she heard raised voices on the other side of the glass wall. The argument appeared to be getting closer.

She tucked away her paperback—bought at a used bookstore for less than two dollars—and pretended to look alert. When the door swung open, she was ready.

A tall man with an angry expression entered, flanked by Julio, who was wearing one of the new T-shirts. They were accompanied by a very tall woman with a no-nonsense expression. Helga was not someone to trifle with before she'd had her coffee in the morning. Or anytime for that matter.

The stranger causing the kerfuffle sported a luxurious mane of platinum hair that flowed past his shoulders and was held back by the tiniest of braids wrapped around his temple. When he got close, she noticed his eyes were the bright green of spring. He wore a very pale gray suit that fit his frame quite nicely. It complemented the feathery white wings popping up from behind his shoulders.

"Hello, sir. Can I help you?" Posie asked nicely.

He ignored her, but he had a harder time ignoring Julio when he threw himself in front of his path. "For the last time, you have no business here."

"I'll ascertain that for myself if you don't mind." The stranger swept Julio aside hard enough that he stumbled.

She'd like to see him lay hands on her. She planted fists on her hips. "Excuse me, but we don't allow the physical handling of our employees. Please kindly conduct yourself as a gentleman."

"Is that a human talking to me?" His brows rose high enough to almost meet his hairline.

"Yes, I'm talking to you. You will apologize to Julio right now."

"I will do no such thing. How dare you speak to me in such a way. And how is it you can see me?"

"I can see you because you're standing right in

front of me. Now, I don't know who you're supposed to be. Perhaps a seagull? Whatever the case, you will kindly behave yourself while you're here."

"A seagull!"

Judging by his indignant expression, she might have guessed wrongly at his costume.

"ALBATROSS?" she offered. "I get them mixed up."

"Did you just insult me?" The man drew himself tall. Who knew green eyes could appear so cold?

"She did," was Julio's snicker.

Posie hastened to correct the misassumption. "No, I was not insulting him." Not entirely true, but never admit to being rude to a customer out loud. "What are you supposed to be then? Perhaps a dove? Your wings are too big for an ostrich."

"I am not a *bird.*" The very word appeared to taste sour to him.

She, on the other hand, managed the sweetest smile. "Let me try again. I'm guessing it should be obvious." She tapped her chin. "Male harpy?"

Someone sucked in a sharp breath, and it occurred to her that she wasn't being very nice. But there was something about this man that rubbed her wrong. He wasn't just rude; condescension oozed from him.

Unacceptable. Being Canadian didn't give him the right to treat her like the gum on the bottom of his shoe sticking to the pavement every time he took a step. If he couldn't treat her with respect, then she'd show him how that felt.

By the scowl on his face, he didn't enjoy it.

Julio turned away, and his body shook as if he were having a fit, whereas Helga appeared so stoic she might have been a statue.

A sneer pulled Mr. Seagull's lips. "I guess I should make allowances given you're only an ignorant human."

"You might want to read up on the definition of ignorant," she muttered.

"You should be kneeling in respect before me. I am an angel, descended from Heaven." He spread his hands and raised his gaze, attempting to look beatific.

It made her giggle because it was so ridiculous. "Sure, you are."

"You doubt my word?" His fine brows arched.

"Now she's done it," muttered Helga.

"Oh, shit. Fuck. I wish I was taping this," Julio sputtered.

"You have the wings, but where's the robe? And

everyone knows angels have halos." She circled a finger over her head.

"Not all choose to wear them."

"Or you haven't earned one." The next obvious choice.

It caused him to suck in and widen his shoulders. The wings ruffled rather realistically. "As Heaven's emissary, I am one of the most highly ranked."

"If you say so. I still have my doubts as to the angel thing seeing as how I was always taught they were nice." The implication was understood, and the man recoiled, while Julio outright chuckled.

"Someone really should do something about that tongue of yours. And then explain to me how it is a human can even see my wings. She shouldn't be able to see me at all." Mr. No-Angel glared at Julio.

Julio finally composed himself. "I'm afraid Ms. Ringwald is not into the cosplaying like you and I." Julio winked at her. "She sees right through our shams."

"Sees through it?" Repeated in a musing manner. No-Angel eyed her. "You think I am a human acting a part."

"And really doing a good job staying in persona." She gave him a thumbs-up.

Julio choked while Helga coughed and looked away.

No-Angel cocked his head and peered at her

more intently. "Fascinating. Have you always been able to see under façades? Or did it start at a certain age?"

She frowned. "What are you talking about?"

"You will come with me."

Posie chuckled. "Like heck am I going anywhere with you."

No-Angel puffed out his chest. "You don't get a choice."

"Actually, she does. And she said no." Julio stepped between them. "I think we're done here."

"That is not your decision to make." An insult meant to cut Julio down. "I am here for the Guild Commander."

Meaning Mr. Reaper, and guess what. Deciding who got to see him was her job. She acted as the intermediary between her boss and clients. This intruder didn't appear to be a client.

Mr. No-Angel went to step around Julio. Posie moved to counter him. "Excuse me, but I'm afraid you'll have to stop right there. You don't have an appointment."

"I don't need one. Step out of my way." Firmly said, his hands folded in front of him. Nothing to indicate violence yet the menace oozed. The guy did not like being denied.

"One, you do need an appointment. Two, Mr. Reaper isn't here, so your childish tantrum is being wasted. Three, here at Grim Dating, we have what is known as a safe workplace, which means we can and will receive respect from everyone who enters our building, be they employee or potential client."

"I don't have to respect you, *human.*" Mr. No-Angel vibrated with rage.

"Actually, you do."

"Dirty, beastly—"

She cut him off. "What did I say about using your nice words?"

"Nice words?" Julio leaned against the wall he was laughing so hard while Helga had her arms crossed and appeared more stoic than ever.

"I speak to you as you deserve," No-Angel spat.

"Is this how people who go to Heaven are treated?" she asked. "I have to say, I'm not impressed. I'd rather go to Hell."

"Oh fuck, you did not just say that," Julio exclaimed.

The angel smiled. "As if you were ever making it to Heaven."

The words were meant as an insult, but she sighed in relief. "Thank gawd."

The angel winced.

She smiled. "Now, as I was saying, Mr. Reaper is unavailable this afternoon. If you'll make an appointment—"

"When will he return?"

"I'm afraid that information isn't available."

"Surely you know."

She didn't, but she wasn't about to admit it. "Make an appointment if you wish to guarantee a meeting with Mr. Reaper."

"You will tell me right now when you expect him."

"You're telling me?" She snorted. "I don't take orders from anyone wearing wings." Just a man in a cloak who signed her paychecks.

"You think my wings false?" They spread out impressively. The things they could do these days with the right kind of robotics.

However, she wasn't about to let a guy with an expensive outfit intimidate her. "Very pretty. I'll bet you spent a whole bunch of money on them. Probably because you still live in your mom's basement."

"Actually, he lives in his father's house," Julio said in a low voice.

"It's a palace," No-Angel countered.

"It's not yours," was her counter-counter.

"I have had quite enough of your disrespect." He loomed, wings spread wide enough to shadow her.

She'd had quite enough of his theatrics. "Enough. Put those wings away. Right now! And then march your butt out of here."

"I don't take orders from you."

Posie crossed her arms. "Do I need to call security?"

"Call the commander. I would speak to him now."

She stuck to her guns. "If you want to meet with Mr. Reaper, then you need to make an appointment."

He glared.

She remained steady.

No-Angel snapped his wings shut and stepped forward, menacing her. She didn't budge.

"You will obey me."

"Or what?" she asked sweetly. "Lay a hand on me and I will have you charged with assault."

"By who?"

"The cops, duh." This guy was taking the act way too far.

"How can you be so blind?" No-Angel muttered aloud. "Is she for real?"

"Very much so," Julio said.

He stared at her. "I am real. Touch my wings and you'll see."

"Don't make me have you charged with sexual harassment, too. Now if you're done, please don't return until you have an appointment. Julio will see to it that it's arranged."

"You'll regret this. The Heavenly Consortium is—"

"Come back when you have an appointment." She managed to turn him around and, with a tug of his arm, pulled him to the door held open by a beaming Julio.

"You'll regret this," No-Angel threatened.

"And there you go again, ruining the whole angel thing. You should think about dyeing your feathers black and tacking a 'fallen' on to your roleplaying shtick."

"You dare—?"

She closed the door before he could finish and finally caught Helga sporting a smile. "I don't think I've ever seen one of those sanctimonious pricks put in his place so well. And without any bloodshed. Good job."

Odd how the praise warmed her. Only just over a week here and she felt more valued than she had in eight years with Mr. Kulley.

At five to five, she began gathering her things, assuming she'd be walking to the station. She'd not once believed Brody would return for her. Why would he? She was just his secretary, and she'd made it quite clear they had to keep things professional.

As she left, more than one person saluted her and yelled goodbye. It was strange. She gave short smiles and quick waves as she hastened her steps to the elevator. She wasn't used to any kind of camaraderie at work. She'd barely spoken to most people here, and yet they seemed to be absorbing her in as if she belonged. She just hoped they never expected her to wear the cloak. Every other employee had one. A few she'd mistaken for dresses, but it turned out some of the women had found interesting ways of winding the cloak and pinning it to make the loveliest dresses.

She rode down alone to the ground level. The moment she stepped onto the gray square and glossy tiles of the main entrance, she saw through the vast glass doors just how hard it poured outside. Torrential came to mind. She wanted to sigh, as she could already imagine the wet trudge to her apartment.

"Good night, Ms. Ringwald," said the guard in the hood at the front desk. It wasn't Barney, who filled his robe a bit thicker, but a new one who tipped her a finger salute. She was startled enough to wave back. Did everyone in the place already know her?

"Let me get that for you." Yet another Grim employee, his hood pushed back and his grin engaging, ran for the door to hold it.

"Thank you?" She couldn't help the querying note.

As she went to step through, the car from the morning pulled up to the curb. From the back seat, Brody stepped out, and she finally saw a use for that massive cape.

He held it up, draping it to form an awning and said with a smile, "I told you I'd return."

1 2

Despite her initial welcoming smile, Posie soon returned to her usual polite self. She sat as far away from Brody as possible, hands tucked in her lap, the image of propriety. It made a man want to do naughty things. What would happen if he slid across the seat and into her space?

She might very well jump out of the car.

But what if she was just waiting for him to make a move so she could melt in his arms? Damn him for thinking of her in that fashion. He couldn't help himself. The more he saw her, the more he appreciated her quiet and commanding manner, and the more he—

Would do nothing. As her employer, he shouldn't get involved. Especially given how closely they worked together.

What if he made a move and she rejected him? It would affect their dynamic at work. He'd have to move her to another department because he wasn't sure if he could stand to see her every day and, worse, know that she would never want him. Might even start dating someone else.

Which smacked of jealousy. Fuck.

"I hear you had a visitor this afternoon." Julio had told him all about the angel's encounter with Posie. His friend had been bent over wheezing as he told Brody what happened.

"You should have seen his face when she basically shoved him out of your office. She is fucking amazing."

"She is," Brody had agreed.

Which was why the difficulty in finding her a proper match. No one was good enough for her. Not even Julio. It made him wonder about something Lucifer had said to him that afternoon over a game of golf—because he wasn't busy enough already. Having a ton of work to do didn't mean that he could say no when the Devil called and said, *"Let's play a round."*

The game wasn't just about losing without making it obvious; it was a quasi-interrogation about Posie as well. Basically, why she wasn't fucking anyone yet.

Before Brody could give lame excuses, the Devil

said, "Why don't you make a play for the girl?"

"Woman," Brody corrected, lining up his leg with the carved ivory ball. "And it wouldn't be correct. I am her employer."

"Exactly. Always take advantage of your underlings," Lucifer declared, giving him a shove just as he swung.

The ball veered into the sand pit and promptly got eaten. It was a given that Brody would lose, especially with the Devil cheating every chance he got.

"She's made it clear she wants nothing personal with me."

"Playing hard to get," Lucifer surmised. "Excellent ploy. Especially because it's working. Look at you, harder than petrified stone every time she comes around. Good thing you've got that robe. I should get one because when you tent, you really fucking tent." The Devil leered and held out his hands indicating an impossible girth.

A reaper did not blush, but he did suddenly find his cloak swirling around his head despite a lack of breeze. "I am not interested in Ms. Ringwald."

"Ah, the lies, you know how I love them." Lucifer sighed, huffing a stream of smoke. "You know what's even better than lies? You putting your sausage into her bun."

"Sir!"

"Don't fucking 'sir,' me. It's obvious you have the

hots for the girl. Otherwise, you could have paired her with so many candidates by now. So hop to it before she's pushing up posies."

"It's daisies."

"My version is cleverer given she is a human with a much shorter lifespan than you. Given her time is limited, you should give her the salami a few times, get it out of your system, and then find a minion she can make babies with. And before you say, 'I'm not gonna fuck her'"—Lucifer adopted a high pitch —"know that this is one lie that I am not appreciating. It's not *if* you're going to hook up but a matter of when. The sooner, the better. Tick. Tock." The Devil tapped his wrist, and every single sandpit exploded. As the wriggling worms with mouths on both ends erupted form the ground, the Devil smiled. "Are you staying for dinner?"

Enough to make him forget for a moment only that the Devil was encouraging him to pair up with Posie. But of the reasons he shouldn't…the biggest one was fear of rejection.

Coward. If he didn't want her, then he should stop stalling and set her up with someone. He had all kinds of lieutenants. Suitable matches, except for Anthony. He preferred his partners more masculine.

Julio seemed rather impressed by her. Would Posie like him in return? Smile for him, that rare sunshine that made her glow? Would she let Julio put his hands on her?

I'll slice his arms off...

Oh fuck. He might have a problem.

I'm jealous. And he didn't want to see Posie with someone else.

I want her to be with me.

As the car pulled up to their apartment building, it appeared the rain had stopped and all the street-lights shone, illuminating everything in a soft, warm nimbus. For once the building didn't appear dreary, but rather—

Oh shit. Brody dove out of the car, but he wasn't in time to stop the person on the sidewalk from opening the door on Posie's side.

A slick voice said, "Hello and forgive my abrupt appearance. You are Ms. Ringwald?"

"Who are you?"

Brody already knew and couldn't help his reac-tion. His cloak crept over his shoulders to cover his head. He slammed shut the car door before she could remark on it. It put him standing tall enough to see the angel on the other side. A man with ridiculously intricate blond hair, a rugged face, and square body.

He cast a pleasant smile at Brody, winked, and then leaned over to introduce himself to Posie. "My name is Raphael, Ms. Ringwald, and I'm here to apologize for my colleague's behavior earlier this afternoon."

"And who's going to apologize for yours?" she muttered. "Move away, please. You're a stranger who is awfully close, and I don't like it."

Surprise straightened Raphael, and he shot a glance at Brody across the car.

Her reply had already brought a smirk to Brody's lips, and he mouthed, "Ouch."

For a second, anger flitted across Raphael's face. It turned into a smirk that managed to look devilish and handsome.

Oddly enough, Posie didn't seem impressed. She emerged from the car and took two paces away from Raphael, not at all dazzled by the blond man who so often was the ideal angel portrayed in art.

"Ms. Ringwald, if we could—"

She sliced a hand to shush him. "No, I am the one who gets to ask questions since you're accosting me. How do you know where I live?"

"Heaven keeps tracks of all the souls on Earth."

Her arms crossed, and her whole attitude screamed unimpressed. "That is not an acceptable answer. My address is not something that is available to the general public, meaning you used back-door methods to access it."

"I'm sorry if my methods of seeking you out were unorthodox."

"This goes beyond unorthodox, and you know it. This is stalking."

"What else could I have done to extend my sincerest—"

She sliced a hand through the air. "You know what you could have done? Sent me an email. Left a voicemail. Heck, you could have sent flowers to me with a note. Tomorrow. At the office. You know, the place where I work."

"I didn't feel this could wait."

"Implying your friend's rudeness was more important than my privacy. It's not, by the way. I hate to break it to you, but you and your weird friend mean nothing to me. I really couldn't care less if you both like to dress up and pretend you're angels. It's quite obvious, given your boorish attitudes, that you should have gone in the other direction. Maybe you can get those wings spray painted another color. Glue on some horns. You could probably use a few tough piercings, too. You know, to give you a more rugged appearance."

Brody got a glimpse of the spunk that so impressed Julio. She was awesome, especially since her tone didn't appear angry. But the disdain...it was quite eloquent.

Brody snickered.

"Are you implying—" Raphael began, but again, she cut him off.

"You are more devils than angels. And I am done dealing with you. I will tell you the same thing I told your friend. Make an appointment. During business hours. I'm currently off duty, so if you'll excuse me." She swept past them both, chin held high and full of attitude.

Raphael's gaze turned from astonishment to admiration. The glow intensified one hundred times and oozed from every pore as Raphael breathed her name in a seductive purr. *"Ms. Ringwald."*

She half turned as she pulled on the door to the building. "If you're going to be a nuisance, I will call the cops."

"Just one question, if you please, and then I promise to run all future correspondence through your place of employment until you give me permission to do otherwise."

"What?" she huffed in clear exasperation.

"When you look at me, what do you see?"

"The person keeping me from my supper and a new rom-com I've been waiting for."

"Do you see wings?"

She rolled her eyes. "Kind of hard to miss them. Good job on getting a bigger set than your friend's."

"Do you see anything else?" he asked, and Brody had to wonder what Raphael was trying to find out.

"The fiery halo is a tad much. Goodbye." She entered the building.

Her last remark was stunning and funny as fuck. "I guess you were just told."

"She sees me and still doesn't believe in me. How does that happen?" Raphael asked.

It was Brody who knew the answer because he'd finally dug into her past. "From a young age, she told her parents what she could see. Her parents thought she was imagining things, so they took her to doctors, which led to pills. Lots and lots of pills. Eventually, she reached an age where she could control her own meds. She went off them, started seeing things, and became convinced it was just the cosplay culture she could see. People dressing up and acting as if it were normal."

"She sees everyone as they are. How incredible. And in such a lovely package."

"Pity angels aren't allowed to date." Brody couldn't help a mocking grin.

The grin wiped when Raphael said, "Who said anything about dating her."

13

THE KNOCK on her door wasn't exactly unexpected. A peek showed Brody standing there, and she could just imagine what he'd say. Probably, *"You're fired."*

She might even deserve it. She'd been rude to that client this afternoon. And then to that Raphael person downstairs. Her defense that they'd started it might not go over well.

What was wrong with her? She'd always been the polite lady. The nice one. And then she got her stupid fortune read a few years ago.

"You'll be in the arms of Death before you're thirty-seven."

A stupid statement from a fake psychic. It meant nothing. She didn't believe in the supernatural. But then there were the other things the fortuneteller predicted that came true.

"They'll come out with pumpkin spice cookie and eggnog cream-filled Oreos."

Crazy, right? Until she'd seen a commercial for it.

"A new island will rise in the Atlantic by Newfoundland."

Again, so unlikely. Until one morning, after a week of winds and fog on the North American east coast, the air cleared and a new isle sprinkled with ruins sat a mile offshore.

And now the most recent proof.

"You will meet an angel."

She'd run into a pair today. How many more clues did she need before she admitted that perhaps the last prophecy would come true?

Her birthday was in two weeks. She'd turn thirty-seven. If something were going to happen, it would be soon. But just in case it didn't, she really should try and keep her job so she could continue to pay rent. And eat.

Time to face the music.

She opened the door. Brody's cape swirled around his shoulders, and the hood appeared more of a cowl than usual, bunching up around his neck as if it wanted to hide his face. Not for the first time, she wondered about the fabric. It never seemed to sit still, the material always vibrating. A suitable outfit for a guy who pretended he was...

The sudden explosion of light bulbs in her head almost rocked her.

I'll be in the arms of death. Could she have misinterpreted the prophecy? Was Brody supposed to be the arms it spoke of? Heck, it could be anyone at Grim Dating for that matter. They all dressed like Grim Reapers.

"Can I help you?" she asked.

For a second, he opened his mouth as if he'd speak. Then closed it.

The hesitation could mean only one thing. "You're trying to tell me I'm fired." She sighed. "I understand. I'm sorry. I don't know what came over me."

"No, you are not fired. Why would you even think that?" he blurted out. "Watching you handle Raphael was actually the most amazing thing I've ever seen. If you ask me, I think you deserve a raise."

"For insulting a potential client?"

"For putting him in his place. The rules forbid me from acting too plainly; therefore it was extremely enjoyable to watch."

"Rules? Is he some kind of competitor?" It would explain a lot.

"In a sense, yes." He shifted, his robe undulating as if agitated. Did he have a fan under there stirring the fabric?

"So I'm not in trouble?"

He shook his head.

"Or fired?" She wanted that clarified.

"No."

"Thank you for letting me know. I guess I will see you at the office in the morning." Making it clear she would make her way there without his aid. It was for the best.

He remained in the doorway, not moving.

"Was there something else?"

"Yes, actually. I realize we are in an awkward position. I am your employer. However, I feel I should mention that I am extremely attracted to you."

"Oh." She didn't have the ability to say anything else. The statement proved startling and titillating.

"I, of course, won't act upon it, and yet, I did feel as if I should let you know. I'll understand if you'd prefer to work in a different department or even leave me to work elsewhere, with a generous settlement, of course."

"You don't want me as your secretary anymore?"

"No. I do want you, that's the problem. You've made it very clear we are colleagues only."

Every chance she got, which made it odd that she felt a need to say, "Your employee handbook has a loose policy about workplace relationships."

"We have a handbook?" Definite surprise in his tone.

"Yes. Not a very big one. I don't think HR gives it out often, given it took them two days to send it to me and it's pasted into an email."

"What does it say?"

He didn't ask her why she'd even gone looking for policies on workplace relationships. A good thing because he was the reason why. "The handbook says nothing because you have no policy on friendships within the workplace."

"What does it say about lovers?" He leaned against the doorway, not coming inside, but definitely flirting.

Her lips rounded. No mistaking what he suggested. "It says nothing at all."

"But it would be a bad idea, right?" he asked.

"Most definitely." She licked her lips. His gaze tracked it and smoldered.

"I still want to kiss you," he admitted.

"Then kiss me." She gave him permission. Because she wanted it, too. Not only was she curious if he was the final prediction, but she'd been fighting her attraction to him for much too long.

His arm wrapped around her waist and drew her near. His lips almost tickled her skin as he said, "I've been fantasizing about you for much too long."

His lips slanted over her mouth and took command of it. He possessed her thoroughly, the hard press of his mouth making her pant. The hard curl of his arm aligning her firmly against him. Firm enough she didn't doubt his interest.

At the insistent probing of his tongue, she parted her lips, and he swept in, plundering her mouth. Making her shiver. Moan. Every sensual touch only served to ignite her further.

His hands stroked up and down her body, stopping to cup her ass. With a growl, he gripped her tight and lifted her, walking her back into her apartment and propping her against the nearest wall.

A first for her. Very hot.

She twined her arms around his neck and held him close, not that she feared falling. His body pinned her in place, ground against her. And she shuddered.

This was the passion she'd always wondered about. The crazy, enflaming need that didn't care that they worked together or that her fateful birthday approached. She barely noticed as he inched up her skirt and palmed her thigh, the leather he wore warmer than expected on her skin. Strange but exciting, too.

He hiked her leg and placed it around his hip. It exposed her more fully to him. Allowed him to grind against her.

She caught her breath. He kept kissing her, devouring her mouth as if she were the tastiest thing. She kissed him back just as hard because he was.

He anchored an arm around her waist and used his free hand to reach under her blouse and cup her breast. He stroked her nipple through the fabric of her bra. Making it peak. Tingle.

He growled against her mouth before moving his way across her jaw then down the column of her neck. The roughness of the shadow on his flesh scraped along her skin.

He nuzzled the fabric in his way, and then somehow that pesky shirt was gone. He'd managed to Houdini it off , leaving her in a bra, the nipples protruding.

Again, he uttered that sexy noise before he plucked a bud with his lips, teasing it, sending jolts of intense pleasure right down to her pussy.

She panted, wishing she had the nerve to ask for more. Every suck and tug on her nipple made the need between her legs only worse.

She whimpered.

He paused then continued his slow suck of her nipple, but the hand loosely placed on her waist slid between their bodies, cupped her sex, with his gloves still on.

"Do you ever take those off?" she murmured.

"No." What he said, and yet he removed the glove

and touched her again. Did he feel how wet she was through her panties?

He pushed the fabric aside and slid a finger into her.

She gasped.

He slid in a second and stroked her, all the while tugging on that nipple. In and out, he thrust steadily with his fingers, and she panted, arched, clawed as his shoulders as the tension inside her tightened. Squeezed so very tight.

When she came, she couldn't help but scream, her body exploding with pleasure. Pulsing and hot. Then languorous as his strokes slowed.

But he didn't stop. He stroked her with his fingers as his lips found hers for a sweet kiss, working her until she writhed against him again, pushing her hips hard against his hand. Wanting more.

Only he pulled away. "I'm sorry. I have to go."

"What?" She had a hard time forcing her heavy lids open. Then an even harder time grasping why he set her down. She braced herself against her wall, trying to understand why he was in the doorway. "Are you leaving?"

"I've got a meeting to attend."

But what about his needs? Her gaze dropped below his waist.

He growled. "Trust me, I'd rather stay here and finish what we started."

That made two of them.

Despite what they both wanted, he left, closing the door softly behind him.

He seriously freaking left. She leaned against the wall a moment longer, catching her breath, feeling the throb between her legs, trying to figure out what had happened. How had it gone from crazy passionate to him practically racing off?

What did it mean?

And what was that funny burning smell in her apartment?

14

BRODY THROBBED. Fiercely. He wanted nothing more than to slip into Posie's welcoming heat, only an insistent tug drew him away. Someone yanked on his reaper contract, summoning him despite his wishes, and not because of a death. As he stepped from the mortal plane into the ether, his mission came to him as a thought.

Come to Hell. Now.

He couldn't ignore the call, which meant leaving more aroused than he'd ever been in his life—and unlife. After almost a century of celibacy, what kind of cruelty was it to pull him away at this precise moment?

Frustration—and the sorest of blue balls—might have made his stalking through the rip in space a little more ominous than usual. His cloak, fully extended, swirled and undulated, a living thing of smoke and shadows.

The question that did circulate in his oxygen-deprived brain was who summoned him? It seemed unlikely the Lord of Hell would have cockblocked him so heinously. On the contrary, Lucifer would have probably wanted to watch. Who else did that leave?

He landed in front of his guild.

Not mine anymore.

That became quite clear as his steps slowed to a stop outside of the building. He spent a bit of time gaping.

Under his hood, he might have shed a tear or two as he beheld the once drab façade painted purple. Not a dark, menacing version but a light, airy violet.

Dread in his step, he entered and uttered a sincere, "What the fuck?" as he saw the Sherpa rugs on the floor, the wicker table and chairs that replaced the previous trestle and benches, and the vines strung with scented and colorful blooms.

Bambi's interior design had transformed the Grim Guild into something delicate and pretty. A fancy indoor garden.

It was almost enough to make him walk off the edge into the abyss. Only remembering how Posie pulsed around his fingers kept him moving forward.

His platform had acquired a set of gold spiral steps leading to a—gulp—pink boudoir.

Thankfully the Devil's daughter didn't force him into the pink monstrosity he used to call home. She held reign, perched on a stool, hand outstretched for someone to buff her nails while another person handled her toes.

"You rang?" he uttered in a low timbre that vibrated.

Blonde hair coiled atop her head, with fat ringlets escaping, his new boss pursed ruby-red lips. "I did page you, and look at you, running to do my bidding like a good reaper, leaving little Miss Posie high and dry. Very cruel, I might add."

No point in asking how she knew. This was Lucifer's daughter. If it involved sex, she could sense it.

"What do you want?" he bit off tersely.

"What I want is for a certain god of war to step up and take care of my needs before I decide I'd rather see him as a crushed tin can," she said on a low growl that turned into a smile. "Such a tease, my sweet War is. The longer the wait, the bigger the orgasm. Right?"

Given how he felt at the moment, he couldn't disagree, which was why he'd like to return to the mortal plane as soon as possible. "I'm kind of on a schedule," he said, lying and doing his big boss proud.

"Always working. If you weren't so obsessed with doing your job well, it would almost be nauseating," she said, sounding almost like her father. "Given your work is about pimping out demons to humans, and you're about to tup your secretary, it would seem you're doing the Dark Lord proud. Which means I am kicking ass as your boss. Yay, me!" She fist-pumped, her eyes alight with a maniacal gleam.

Perhaps someone should send this War fellow a note about doing everyone a favor and putting out a certain fire. He'd never heard any hints of Bambi being violent like other past members of the Baphomet family. However, he didn't get the impression she abstained often.

"Yes, you are doing quite well." He had to keep his gaze off the décor to say the words with a straight face.

"I am, which is why nothing can screw up. I'm tired of my father always ditching me for the newest flavor. Siblings are overrated."

"I thought you liked your younger sister, Muriel." He'd seen a few hellocumentaries that showed them together.

"Little lamb has grown up and doesn't have much time for me anymore." Her lips turned down. "People are always moving on." Her lips suddenly tilted. "Moving on is great. You never get tired of that week's flavor."

"Seems tiresome," he observed. "Much easier to be alone."

"I don't find it easy at all. And I'll bet Posie doesn't like it either."

A jab that had him changing the subject. "Is there anything else you needed me for?" He had other things he'd prefer to attend to.

"I heard some angels visited you today."

He should have known she'd want to discuss it. "Only one angel technically. I missed the first because I was playing golf with your father."

"That first visitor was to your secretary, the girl who sees all. Which is kind of disturbing." Bambi patted her wild blonde curls.

"Does everyone know about her ability?" Because she seemed to be getting an awful lot of attention suddenly.

Bambi smirked. "Funny how it happens. A person hides under our noses for the longest time, and suddenly, dear old Dad gets involved and their life turns into a clusterfuck. The annoying, not hole-stuffing, kind."

"What does that mean now that others are aware of her ability?"

"She'll probably get offers."

"That she won't believe." He paced, his cloak

swirling, a living smoke that would wrap him like a shield if threatened. People often assumed reapers were invulnerable, comprised of incorporeal shadow. The truth? They remained flesh and blood. The cloak was their armor. It protected, healed, kept them alive. But as with any shield, batter it enough and it would be torn to tatters.

"I don't think she'll be able to pretend for much longer. She's been weaning off her pills."

"She still takes medication?"

"A bit of a cocktail, but the good news is most have been replaced for placebos. Except for the water retention. That shit is amazing at dealing with bloat." Bambi patted her belly. Flat, her waist cinched, her hips flaring. She went for a voluptuous style.

He preferred Posie's shape. Perfect

"Is there a way we can hide her?" he asked.

"I think she has been hidden these past thirty some years."

"By magic?"

Bambi shrugged. "Doesn't matter. It's gone now, and there are people asking about her."

"What people?" It hit him a second later. "You mean the angels. What did they say?"

"I'll get to that in a moment. First, we need to discuss some recent business developments. Namely, Heaven's legal department sent a cease and desist in regard to the matchmaking operation. We, of course, refused to comply. Rather eloquently, too. My father sent back the messenger's hand in a box, middle finger extended."

That would send quite the message.

"How did they reply?

"How do you think?" was her sarcastic drawl. "They were more pissed than a nest of hornets being shaken. They said we'll crush you, blah, blah." She waved a hand. "We said bring it mother fuckers. Which made more than a few cry." She snickered. "Apparently that kind of affection is a sin. Which led to the Dark Lord offering to buy them some hookers that they might, and I quote, 'Drain their holy balls so they would stop being so uptight.'"

"Is he trying to start a war?"

"We thought he was," Bambi admitted, holding up her manicured nails for an admiring peek. "He had the legions marching up Main." Main was a road that bisected all the rings. "Did a speech, fire, brimstone, and let's kick some ass."

"He threatened them? But we don't have the numbers to take on Heaven right now." The whole purpose of Grim Dating was to increase the usable population in Hell.

"The boneheads running Heaven are dumb as fuck. They believed our bluff, but they couldn't back down, so Lucifer suggested a wager that avoids an all-out skirmish."

That didn't bode well. "What kind of wager?"

"The kind that leads me back to the lady you left panting and wet. Posie's ability to *see* has drawn the attention of the archangels. They are very interested in her."

Fucking Raphael. Couldn't handle the rejection. "They can't have her," Brody growled.

Bambi arched a brow. "As if that was your choice."

"She's not an object you can use for bargaining," he argued.

"I agree. Which is why the wager has to do with *her* choice." Bambi stressed the pronoun.

"What's that supposed to mean?"

"It means that the winning side will be decided by whomever Posie chooses."

"I don't understand. What are her choices?"

"You or Raphael, of course. Who will be the one to win her heart?"

His stopped. "You're talking about love."

"Yes, love, that emotion you keep pretending doesn't exist. And maybe for you it doesn't. Which would suck because the terms of the wager are if Posie declares her love to someone on our side, Grim Dating remains open for business and Heaven won't interfere."

"And if she doesn't fall in love with me?"

"Actually, it doesn't have to be you, specifically. Just someone playing for our side. If we lose, then we agree to shut down all matchmaking operations on the mortal plane, plus no visitation privileges for anyone for the next ten years. And by no visitation, that includes reapers. Everyone would be Hellbound for that decade."

"But the dead…"

"Will haunt the living for a while. Ten years isn't horrible. Unless there's some kind of catastrophic event."

"What of Lucifer's need to rebuild the army?"

"We'll still make babies. It just won't be as easy. But you are talking as if we're going to lose. Ha. As if. We're already halfway there, judging by the smell of pussy on your fingers."

Sex didn't equal emotion. It was physical need. "She doesn't love me."

"Perhaps not yet. But it won't take much."

"I don't want her to love me." A lie. And he didn't even realize it until the words emerged from his mouth.

"Then make sure she loves someone else playing for our team. I don't care who it is, just so long as those angelic jerks don't win."

In order for the other side to lose, Posie had to fall in love.

With someone.

And when he got home, hours later, because he got roped into paperwork, he began thinking about who that someone could be. His mind kept saying, *Me.*

15

POSIE EXPECTED a knock at her door, but when it didn't come by eleven, she went to bed. Got up too early with circles under her eyes and penned a letter of resignation. She'd had a good chunk of last night to think about it.

She couldn't continue to work for him. He'd never respect her.

Heck, she wasn't sure she could respect him. The passion that had been simmering finally overflowed. With it now unbound, could she control herself around him, or would she turn into that pathetic girl who threw herself at the boss?

She had to quit. She had the letter explaining her decision tucked in her purse as she entered the hall seven minutes later than usual. Despite having peeked, she'd not seen him waiting.

"Good morning." His low timbre shivered over her skin. He wore his cloak over his body, but the hood remained down, his expression serious.

"Hi." She had no idea what to say and felt rather awkward. How did one handle a morning after when you weren't quite sure of your feelings —or his?

"My apologies for my abrupt departure last night. My business detained me longer than expected."

"No need to apologize." The polite thing to say and yet she appreciated his words. "Do you often have after-hours meetings?"

"Unfortunately. My boss expects me to be at her beck and call, day or night."

"She?" The word slipped out before Posie could stop it.

"Yes, she. I assume you'll meet her soon. She likes to stick her nose in everything. Just don't let her redecorate the office if I'm not around. She is abnormally fond of pastel colors."

Her lips quirked. "I'll keep that in mind."

"Have dinner with me tonight," he asked. "I know a place that makes excellent pasta."

"Um." If she said no, he'd think she was rejecting him, but she honestly didn't know if she could sit a few hours across from him and make conversation when she couldn't stop thinking of—

His expression smoldered suddenly. "On second

thought, maybe we should eat in. I don't know if I want to share you."

Those words melted her. Her hand shook slightly as she locked her door.

He slid close. "Are you cold?" He placed an arm around her, tucking her into him, his cloak spreading over her and filling her with heat.

"Brody..." Now was the time to tell him.

"I haven't been able to stop thinking about you," he softly murmured against the hair covering her ear.

It sent a shiver through her. She turned in his arms. "I've been thinking of you too, but..."

"But what?" he asked, moving close, leaning over her so she had to look up.

"You and me. It's inappropriate." She huffed hotly, her heart pounding at how close his mouth hovered.

"Not according to the handbook."

"I should quit."

"No."

"You can't say no. This is wrong."

"We'll make it work."

The intenseness of the conversation had her laughing nervously and turning from him. "Speaking of work, we should go, or we'll be late."

"My car is waiting downstairs."

When she moved by rote to the elevator, his hand

rested on the hollow of her back. Just a simple touch. It warmed her to her toes.

He helped her into the car and slid in right after her rather than going around, forcing her to scoot. Not far, as he grabbed her hand and laced his fingers with hers.

"Didn't we just talk about this being—"

"Right? Because I thought we'd both ascertained last night that there is an undeniable spark between us."

What could she say? He spoke the truth. Arousal filled her every time she remembered his touch. She couldn't admit she had pathetically hoped he'd come over. She'd hoped the throb would be gone this morning, and then she saw him.

The spot between her legs pulsed.

This would be longest day ever.

"Something wrong?" he asked softly.

How to explain that she wanted him to touch her?

It was as if he read her mind. "Come here," he growled as he pulled her into his lap. She gasped. He caught the sound with his lips, tugging them and sucking on the flesh. "I've been wanting to do this since you opened that door."

She couldn't help but sigh in pleasure. Which led to more kissing and squirming. No mistaking his arousal. It pressed against her bottom, and for a fleeting, insane moment, she wished she'd worn a skirt. It would have been easy to straddle him and... what? Have sex with him in the car while being driven by someone she'd yet to meet?

Did the driver watch? She froze.

"What's wrong?"

She moved off of him, cheeks flushed. "We can't do this here."

"Then where?" The car slowed, and Brody offered her a wink. "My office."

"Oh." The thought just made the pulse between her legs worse. "That's not a good idea. We can't have sex while we're working."

"Why not?" he asked.

"Because if you're paying me, then that makes me a whore."

He blinked. "So I won't pay you."

"Which doesn't help my bills. Meaning the smarter move is no sex, because I need a paycheck to keep my electricity."

"How about we fine-tune that to no sex at the office? Then that would make us two consenting adults indulging in their free time."

A rule about sex. What was happening? Why was she behaving in such a manner?

He dragged her in for a kiss, flustering her and reminding her why.

Because he made her catch on fire.

She pulled away breathless. "We're late."

"I'm wishing we'd stayed home." He looked as frustrated as she felt.

Perhaps she should have stuck to her guns and quit. This would be the longest day ever.

Entering the building, she felt as if everyone watched them, and her cheeks turned hot. What would they think of her if they knew what had happened? Then again, how would anyone know? Unless the driver told.

No one said anything, and the moment she entered her sanctum she let out a breath that had him chuckling.

"Why so nervous?"

"I don't want your staff judging me. Us."

"Is there an us?" He drew her close.

"I guess we'll find out." After work. When she was off the clock.

They separated as the door opened. Julio entered, his lips tilted in a knowing grin. "So, how's it going?"

"Fine."

"Just fine? Don't let Brody hear you." He winked.

She wanted to hide.

The subtle, and not so subtle, hinting happened all day long and was compounded by Medusa's scowl, which wasn't to say she was typically nice. She was just nastier today than usual. Or did she imagine it?

How could everyone know about her and Brody? Was he bragging to everyone?

If she'd worried that Brody might try and advance their relationship at work, she shouldn't have. Once they were inside the office, he'd remained courteous. Flirty and smiling when they were alone but the epitome of professional when they weren't.

She'd have wondered if she'd imagined the passion of that morning if every now and then she didn't catch a glimpse of him staring at her hungrily.

Longest day ever.

The flowers arrived midafternoon. A bouquet of white roses with a note.

Have dinner with me.

Hadn't she already said yes?

She knocked sharply on Brody's office door.

"Enter."

She walked in waving the card. "Yes, I'll have dinner with you. Thanks for the flowers."

"What flowers?" he asked.

"The bouquet that arrived," she said, only to realize by his expression he truly knew nothing about it.

"I wish I had sent you flowers. Who are they from?" He bristled as he came around her desk. Angry because someone sent her flowers?

It seemed impossible. She'd never inspired jealousy before.

"I don't know." She turned the card over and saw it was embossed with wings.

"Fucking Raphael," he growled.

The name arched her brows. "The guy from the sidewalk?"

"Yeah, him."

"That was nice of him to send flowers." Not really, but she was strangely fascinated by Brody's reaction.

"You will not encourage him."

She blinked. "Excuse me? Are you telling me what I can do?" Not cool and yet hot all at once.

"No. Yes. Maybe." He ran a hand through his hair. His agitated pacing caused his cloak to swirl. "I don't want you to see him."

"I'd say that's my choice."

"I thought we were dating."

"I don't know what we are, but even if we were, you don't get to tell me what to do."

"Think of it as me warning you then. Raphael isn't being honest."

"What does dinner have to do with honesty?"

"He's only asking you out because I'm interested in you."

"That seems like an egocentric theory, given you only declared your interest after I met Raphael." Her eyes widened. "Wait. Is that the only reason you seduced me?"

"I did it because I want you."

"Do you? Or is it because seeing another man show interest in me bothers you?"

"Of course, it bothers me," he barked. "I don't want anyone touching you but me."

A hot declaration and yet now she had to wonder. Did he like her, or was he trying to take her away from someone else? What would happen if Raphael stopped showing interest? Would he move on? "I don't think we should see each other after work."

"Why not?"

"Because I'm not some quick and easy conquest. Some notch in an ego contest you have going with your rival." She lifted her chin. "I also resign."

"Posie..."

She shook her head. "No. This was a bad idea. I should have never come in this morning. We can't work together." Head held high, she marched out of his office. Right out of the building. And back to her apartment where she had a good sob. Then some ice cream, because sugar fixed everything.

He didn't call.

Or knock.

Because he didn't care.

Which took bacon to feel somewhat better about.

That afternoon she got a friendship request on social media from—guess who—Raphael Angellus. Stalking her again.

She ignored it.

Ding.

He sent a private message.

She thought about deleting it unread. Even had her finger over the button to click when she read the first line. *There's something you need to know about Brody Reaper. He's—*

The message cut off, meaning she'd have to open it to read the rest. Did she care?

Click.

It loaded, and as she read the whole missive, she gaped. Read it again. Snorted. Then got mad.

This was taking things too far.

And despite knowing the stupidity in confronting Brody while high on sugar and dumb due to brain freeze, when she heard his door lock beeping, she whipped open hers as fast as she could and snapped, "Did you actually make a wager over who would get in my pants first?"

16

HE'D WONDERED all day what he could do to fix things with Posie. Now there she was, madder than before, and somehow aware of the wager with Heaven. Blaming him for it. Her soul seethed. He had to fix this.

"It wasn't my idea."

Her eyes widened. "But you knew about it. This wasn't just some rivalry thing for you. You actually made a bet!"

"Not me! My boss did."

"The woman you met with last night?"

"Not her, my other boss. The big boss."

"Why the heck is anyone making a wager that involves me? And one that involves sex? That is so disgusting."

"It wasn't about sex."

"But it did have to do with seducing me, and like a good employee, you went right to it."

"I will have you know I seduced you before the wager was made." His lame defense.

"And that's supposed to make it all right?" She came into his space, livid, her body bristling. She'd never been more beautiful.

Never more deadly.

A reaper didn't usually feel any pain. He'd already lived and died. While his body could be damaged, it didn't happen often, given he used the magic of his cloak to dissipate before painful contact. However, he had no protection for his emotions. In a short span, this woman had managed to worm her way into his life, his mind, and his long-dead heart.

But this wasn't just about him. Her feelings mattered to him. And right now, she was hurt and hated him. He had to fix this somehow. "There's things you don't know. Things about me and Raphael, even the company, that I can't tell you."

She arched a brow.

He amended, "I shouldn't tell you, mostly because I doubt you'll believe me."

"Why don't you try?"

"I know you see us as we are. And before you say anything, we're not cosplayers. At least most of us aren't. I'm real. So are the reapers at Grim Dating. Our clients. Even the angels."

Her scowl deepened. "This isn't funny. Don't you make this about your delusion."

"It's not a delusion. Heaven and Hell are real. That's where I'm from. Hell, that is. Sixth ring. I was commander of the Canadian Reaper Guild until my new assignment."

"As a matchmaker?" She snorted. "You couldn't even sell this concept if you tried. It's completely unbelievable."

"What will it take to convince you that we are real? That what your parents and those doctors taught you was wrong. They couldn't see what you do. You, and only you, see past the magic."

"What do you know of my parents?" Her nostrils flared.

"That they didn't understand just how special you are."

"Seeing things made me special all right." Her lips turned down. "And I thought I was cured. I hadn't seen anything until I went to see that psychic. Then I was a kid all over again, telling my parents about the gargoyle walking down the street. They made me apologize and sent me for sensitivity and cultural training." Because apparently what she saw was a racist projection.

"You're not crazy."

"Because you're real?"

"We're not actors playing dress-up."

"Then prove it."

"How?"

"Take someone's soul. Right now. Yank out your knife, scythe, whatever, and reap a ghost."

"I can't."

"Because you're not real."

"No, I can't because a reaper can only take souls he's been assigned."

Her nose wrinkled. "You have an answer for everything, don't you?"

"How about I show you something else."

"You said you come from Hell. Show me."

"I can't. Only the dead and demonic can cross the planes. Humans are forbidden."

"A likely excuse."

He grabbed her close. "It *is* the truth, much as my Dark Lord hates it when I use it."

"You can't show me because it's not real," she exclaimed. "None of you are real." She put hands to her heads and closed her eyes. "I'm sick."

It roused anger in him and compassion. Time to free her that she might finally know the truth. "Posie, my prickly flower," he purred. "Look at me. Look upon the reaper of souls. The final thing seen before judgment.

As she faced him, her cheeks stained in tears, he let his cloak swirl, losing the leash he had on it. The agitation coursing through him rippled the esoteric fabric, showing her his deadly glory. Scythe and all.

And still she didn't believe.

So he clutched her close and took her into the other place. The place of nothingness. And as she gazed into the space between the realms, she gasped. Then went still as he offered her the briefest glimpse of Hell. A quick in and out. Enough to smell the burning ash and feel the heat.

They reappeared in his living room.

Features frozen, she said stiffly, "Did I eat something? Magical mushrooms? Acid?"

"No."

She eyed him. "You really are Death?"

"Not quite. I'm a reaper. I take souls to their next destination."

"I see." For a moment she said nothing, and he wondered at her thoughts. "Is the dating thing a front for the fact you're here doing your job?"

"No, we're not reaping anymore. We truly are matchmakers. Facilitating relations between humans and those from Hell."

"Why?"

"Because the Devil wants to rebuild his army."

That caused her to blink. "You're helping the Devil?"

He shrugged. "Hell isn't what you think."

"What is it, then?"

"It's similar to this world, but without some of the veneer and more rules. The Devil likes his rules."

"I thought he was about anarchy and everything."

"That, too. Rules bring about rule breaking, which is sinning."

"Sin without causing too much harm, he'll turn a blind eye. Start causing havoc that takes him away from his other activities…"

"And the Devil comes down like a hammer."

"You know him personally?"

"He's my boss, but I don't see him too often."

"Have I ever met him?"

"As a matter of fact, yes and no. He was in the elevator with us not long ago, but I don't think you could see him."

"Probably a good thing," she muttered. "If you're real, and everyone I've met at work is too, then those angels…" She gnawed her lower lip. Had she really insulted God's soldiers? Ouch.

"Raphael and Jericho are archangels working at the highest level in Heaven."

"There really is a God?"

"Actually, that's complicated right now. His son is kind of in charge while his dad is in jail, but he's not calling himself anything yet."

"Jesus mutinied against his father?"

"Like I said, complicated."

"Are all angels as rude as them?"

"The way they treated you is standard because, in their minds, humans are beneath them."

"Making them snobs. But if they hate us, then does anyone go to Heaven?"

"Only those pure of spirit."

"Well shit," she muttered. She flopped onto his couch. "This is quite a bit much to take in."

He sat beside her. "You are overwhelmed right now. You'll quickly adjust. I did. It was past time you knew the truth."

"It was easier when I assumed you were all crazy cosplayers."

"Why?"

She offered a wan smile. "Because you're a reaper, and I'm just me."

"I like you."

"Because of a wager."

"Fuck the wager. I don't give a shit who wins it."

"What are Heaven and Hell playing for?"

"Grim Dating's existence."

"Meaning if you lose and they win, everyone is out of a job. No pressure then."

"I won't take advantage of you. I don't care what Lucifer says."

She snorted. "Because you are pals with the Devil."

"Don't even suggest it," he replied with a shudder.

"What's he like?" she asked. "Is he like Hellboy, all big and hulking and red, killing everyone?"

"He usually wears a human guise, without any accoutrements, unless you count his couture. He's highly intelligent, but sly. In many respects, given the amount of sins in the world, he is the most forgiving and at the same time most unrelenting. Meddlesome, too. Thinks he's some kind of Cupid."

"The Devil setting people up?" She laughed. "That's the most ridiculous thing I've ever heard."

"Yet he's apparently quite good at it." After all, Lucifer had been bugging him to go after Posie. If he'd given in to his passion earlier, the wager would have never happened. Meaning the Devil would have bet on something else...

She reached out and stroked a hand over his cloak. It shivered in response. "Do you ever take it off?" she asked of his magical garment. His armor. His identity.

He shook his head. "Part of the transformation bonds us to the robe. It is what gives us our power."

"So you were human once?"

"A long time ago, before my bargain with the Devil."

"How long?"

Rather than reply, he offered her more of the lore. "A reaper would die if they were to lose their cloak. It is bound to our lives. It is our shadow that keeps us from being seen on the mortal plane."

"And the scythe?"

"More of our magic. It takes but a thought to call it forward." He held out his hand and his scythe appeared. "We can change it, too." It turned into a pitchfork then a martingale such as dog handlers used. Regular dogs that was. Hellhounds couldn't be controlled by any but a Baphomet and the kennel master.

"Do you miss being alive?" she asked.

"Not until I met you." How to explain that she made him remember how it could be to feel? To want to be with someone. To live for a smile.

She reached for him, her fingers brushing his cheek. "Can you be with someone?"

He turned his face into her touch. "Yes." In a moment of brutal honesty, he admitted, "But you're the first since my death that I've wanted for more than a night." He wanted eternity, and yet, her mortality was plain to see.

"Why do you look sad?" she murmured, brushing his lower lip.

"Because while you and I can be together for your lifetime, the moment you die…"

"You'll drag me to Hell. How is that bad? You said you lived there."

"I do. However, reapers can't associate with the damned."

"Why not?"

"The magic…" He shrugged. "I don't understand it, only that the souls in hell can't touch us. And once they cross the Styx, they even stop seeing and hearing us."

"Meaning, when I die, it's over." She frowned. "Am I going to die young?"

"I don't know." Rumors had been swirling since the beginning of time that a person's time on Earth left a mark that pinpointed their death. If it did, he couldn't read it.

"A few years ago, I had some psychic tell me that I'd end up in the arms of death before I turned thirty-seven."

"A prophecy," he exclaimed.

"I guess. As some of the other things she said came true, I've been getting more and more anxious the closer my birthday gets. It didn't help that right after seeing her was when I started spotting"—she paused—"non-humans. Up until recently, I thought I was going to die. But now that I've met you, I really wish she'd mentioned death would be so handsome."

She kissed him. It was sweet. Soft.

Forgiving.

He groaned as he let himself touch her, his hands

gripping her by the waist, lifting her to more deeply plunder her mouth.

She uttered a sound, half moan, half passionate need. She held his face as she kissed him right back. They ended up on the couch, him sitting with her in his lap. As his hands roamed her body, she molded herself to him. The tips of breasts pressed into him, her nipples hard nubs. He ground his erection against her bottom. She gasped and squirmed.

It was too much. He had to…

Taste her.

Yes.

He dumped her onto the couch, ignoring her soft protest that he might kneel. Her eyes half-lidded, she watched him as he tugged at her pants, pulling them past her hips and down her legs. Her panties quickly followed.

He parted her knees, exposing her, feeling the heat of her shyness and yet loving the bold demand in her gaze at the same time. Holding it, he dipped until his mouth was level with her sex.

At the first lick of his tongue across her nether lips, she cried out. "Brody."

Oh, how he liked hearing his name on her lips.

He wanted more. He wanted her screaming it. He licked again. And again. Feasted on her, spreading her honeyed lips to lap at her core. He jabbed her with his tongue and flicked her clit.

She moaned and squirmed at his touch. Bucked when he sucked on her swollen button. Stiffened and panted as her pleasure peaked, ready to tilt into climax.

But he was too greedy to finish her with his tongue. Maybe the next time, because there would be a next time.

Right now, he wanted to feel her. To have her come with his cock buried deep. He shoved open his pants, freeing his shaft.

Grasping her by the thighs, he positioned her on the couch, close enough he could rub against her, shuddering at the heated slickness of her sex. Moaning as she reached to grab him.

He might have tortured them both forever if she'd not locked her legs around his waist and drawn him closer, pulling him into her.

Heat. Tight. Wet. Molten. Pleasure.

His head went back as he thrust into her sex. Stretched her with his thick shaft. Felt her clenching him.

"Brody." She panted his name. "Brody…"

She was coming. He wanted to come with her. He slid his hands under each of her cheeks and began to pump her, in and out. Stroking deep. Hard.

Her gasps turning to high-pitched squeaks. Then a cry and shudder as she came, her flesh clutching him, fisting him.

Fuck. It felt... Ah. He kept thrusting and pumping through the tight vise of her sex, keeping the angle that had her gasping.

"I'm going to come again."

And she did, a hard second climax, so hard that he was caught buried to the hilt inside her as her body bowed and held him. Squeezed him until he huffed, "Posie. I—"

He came and lost the words he was going to say.

Came harder than he ever imagined possible.

A century's worth of pent-up ardor.

And yet the second and third times were just as intense. She'd just fallen asleep in his arms when he felt the tug.

"Not now." He groaned.

"What's wrong?" she grumbled in her sleep.

"I'm being summoned."

"Sucks to be you."

"I'll be right back." He kissed her softly.

"M'kay." She snuggled into his pillow and he'd never hated his job more than in that moment.

Which might have been why, when he appeared in Hell, the first thing he barked was, "What the fuck do you want now?"

Posie had barely managed to fall asleep when there was a knock. She tried to ignore it. It proved most insistent.

Rap. Tap. Rap.

She didn't want to answer. This wasn't her apartment. Brody had left, but she had no doubt he'd be back. Call it a gut feeling. After everything he'd shown her, the way he'd worshipped her body... Something had happened between them.

She'd been in the arms of death and loved it!

"Open the door, Ms. Ringwald. We really should talk."

Her eyes popped open at the loud voice. She glanced at the bedroom door almost expecting to see the person.

"We don't have much time."

She pursed her lips. It sounded like the angel Raphael. The same one who'd tried to cause trouble by sending that message. She had a thing or two to say to him.

She took a quick moment to dress but couldn't do much for her hair. Only then did she swing open the door and huff, "Stop harassing me."

"I am merely trying to prevent a grave mistake from happening."

"Too late. You lost. Brody won."

How could such a handsome face be so ugly when it smiled? "He hasn't won yet. The wager wasn't about copulation, but affection. You haven't told him you love him."

"And? I feel it."

"Feelings don't matter. The bet was quite clear."

"Since you're going to whine about technicalities, then fine." She tilted her chin. "As soon as he returns, I'll tell him."

"What a shame that he'll be too late."

"What's that supposed to mean?"

"That you'll never see him again." Handsome features didn't make him appealing, and his words only made it worse. "Shall we go for a ride?"

Raphael reached for her. She tried to evade his grasp, but he proved quick, too quick, and strong.

Burly arms wrapped around her and dragged her from the apartment.

"Let me go." She struggled to escape his grip.

"Not yet. First, I'm going to prove to you just how real I am."

"Will you release me if I say I believe you're an angel?"

"We wouldn't want there to be any doubts." Now that he had a hold of her, he dragged her down the hall to the stairwell, shoving her through and then up the steps, all the way onto the roof.

A few rattling units for air circulation lined the roof. Someone had attempted a bit of outdoor space with strung Christmas lights and mismatched outdoor furniture. Raphael ignored it and dragged her to the parapet.

Would he kill her? Rather than trying to escape, she clung to him as he stood on the lip. "Put me down."

"Haven't you always wanted to fly?" He dove over the edge.

She screamed.

She opened her eyes when she felt a jolt and heard a strange snap. She saw the wings first over his shoulder, massive, beating to draw them upwards.

She wasn't going to die, a meat pancake on the

sidewalk. Yet. She had to find a way to escape the mad angel.

"What are you going to do with me?"

"Do? Nothing now that you've let that reaper taint you. It really is a shame you chose him over me. And without even giving me a chance."

"Is it really worth having a tantrum over it? Killing me won't change the fact I am not interested in you."

"Who said anything about killing you?" Raphael glanced at her. "I'm about to bestow upon you the greatest honor imaginable. I'm taking you to heaven."

"What? No."

"Don't be foolish. This is a rare present I am bestowing. Do you know how many of your kind would do anything to receive this gift?"

"Then give it to someone else. I don't want to go with you."

He ignored her and continued to arrow upwards.

"Let me go."

"We're almost there, where you will live for an eternity. In a cell, unfortunately, as we can't allow someone like you to roam around freely, but better than the alternative."

"I'm supposed to go to Hell."

"Only the dead are taken there. And with Heaven's care, that won't be for a very long time."

Oddly enough he gave her the answer she needed. The way to escape.

Maybe Brody would be there to catch her before she hit.

18

"WHAT THE FUCK do you want now?" Brody yelled into the ash-filled sky of Hell the moment he set foot in it. There was no one there to reply, which didn't improve his ire.

Leaving a warm bed with a naked Posie didn't rate high on his list of things to do. Especially to answer a summons from the Dark Lord.

However, the reaper contract meant he also couldn't say no. He noticed that rather than being summoned to the guild ring, he stood outside the Dark Lord's gate in the first ring, where the most prestigious lived. The castle was directly in the center with no one but the Devil and his wife able to port directly inside.

Upon passing through the rusty gates—not something he did often, and still awe inspiring after centuries in Hades—Brody found himself in a massive courtyard. The distance was quickly crossed, needing only one pace to bring him to the castle steps where a short, bald fellow with scaly green skin waited for him. Polkadot something or other.

Poke-a-butler peered over small round-rimmed glasses, a clipboard in hand. "Name."

"Brody Reaper. I was summoned."

The major domo ran his finger down the parchment before murmuring, "Ah yes. The pimp master."

Brody winced.

"You are right on time. If you would follow me."

Polk-a-butler moved more quickly than expected. Brody had to almost jog to keep up as they wound through a series of hallways and even through some chambers. The artwork on the wall proved detailed and brilliant, some of it moving, others watching. Carved statues were scattered, many of impossible beasts. Eclectic furniture crowded some rooms. A collector gone mad.

Eventually they entered a wide hall with red carpet trimmed in gold, lined with armored statues. Although the occasional shiver of the outfits and creak of a metal joints made him wonder if there was someone inside.

Polk-a-butler gave a brisk knock at a pair of giant battered gold doors before swinging them open. A pair of hellhounds basked in front of a roaring fireplace and turned flame-filled eyes on him.

The Devil's office hadn't changed much since the last time Brody visited. Still some giant skull of a long extinct animal carved as a desk. Violent and yet captivating murals across the walls. Leather-wrapped club chairs, and the Devil, wearing hospital scrubs in a deep red, smoking a cigar.

"There he is, the man of the hour. The defiler of humans. About time."

But Brody wasn't in the mood for the Devil's antics. "What do you want now? I was kind of busy."

"No, you weren't. I waited until you were both worn out before calling. Most excellent job by the way. Despite your long bout of celibacy, you defiled her most profoundly." The Devil proffered a hand-rolled cigar. "Rolled by Castro himself. Even has a few tears."

Brody accepted it but had to say, "I don't need a reward. Even without the bet, I would have ended up with Posie." Because his attraction to her had every-thing to do with the woman herself.

"The cigar is not because of your dicking skills but because of mine. Gaia just birthed me a fine daughter. A man can never have too many, you know. I recommend them as the progeny of choice, as they tend to take longer to turn against their fathers." An odd remark that brought a momentary sad cast to the Devil's face. Ruined by a smirk. "So how was the sex?"

"I'd rather not discuss my relationship with Posie."

"Oh ho, so it's a relationship now." Lucifer smirked. "Take it from me. Run, boy, run, before she snares you in the marriage trap."

Thunder clapped inside the room. Which seemed odd.

The Devil glared at the ceiling. "Bloody wench is always listening. Leave me alone." He shook a fist at the air. "I'm having guy-talk time."

"Did you require something from me, my lord?" It was hard to keep respectful when all he wanted was to return to his apartment.

"I wanted to say that, while I know you tried your hardest, your failure to get the woman to admit her love for you is a disappointment. But in good news, the angels are just as fucked as we are. Once that anti-abortion bill passes, they will slow down their recruiting for a bit."

"Wait, what do you mean lost? Posie and I—"

"Fucked. Yes. I know. And I'm sure had you put the meat to her a few more times, she'd have been emotionally tenderized enough to say the big L word. But alas, we've been outmaneuvered."

A chill filled him. "What are you talking about? I wasn't aware there was a timeframe put in place."

"There wasn't. However, I'm afraid Raphael never was a good loser. And yet do they toss him from Heaven? No. Because he's Elyon's favorite. Which means he'll probably be forgiven again for what he's about to do."

"What is he doing?"

"The thing I'd have expected one of my minions to do if the roles were reversed. Get rid of the woman before she makes them lose a bet to me."

The meaning sank in, and Brody got lightheaded then cold. His cloak rose to smother him head to toe.

"Raphael is an angel. Even he can't murder in cold blood."

"He won't. I imagine his plan to is lock her up somewhere in heaven and forget about her. Perhaps in time, she'll end up falling for the handsome angel. Or not. By taking her out of the game, neither side wins the bet."

"He can't lock her up. I won't let him."

"It's too late."

Brody might have called the Devil a liar, but he felt a sudden tug. A summoning of his reaper for a death, the first since his change in job. Icy fear jolted him as he stepped into the nothing place. The knowledge of whom he went to collect hitting him as he crossed space.

No.

No.

No!

His anguish didn't matter. He'd arrived too late.

Raphael didn't even bother to hide his smirk as he surveyed the mess he'd wrought. "Such a tragedy. I blame her excitement when I told her I was taking her to heaven forever and ever."

"Why you—" Brody swelled, his cloak spreading shadow, his scythe bigger than he'd ever managed before.

Raphael shone bright and sneered. "What will you do, reaper? We both know you're not allowed to touch me."

"You know what the Dark Lord says. Rules are made to be broken."

"And you know the consequences."

He didn't care. Not with Posie dead.

Brody took a step toward the angel, his cloak a ripple of storm and impending doom that suddenly wilted as a tentative voice said, "Brody? Is that you? I knew you'd come."

Posie's soul hovered amidst the wreckage of her mortal body and reached for him, only to have her hand pass right through.

She frowned and waved her fingers through him again. "Brody?"

"I'm sorry, Posie."

"I don't understand. I can see you. Why can't I touch you?" She glanced down, and her eyes widened. "I'm dead!"

"Meaning my job here is done. Enjoy your eternity in hell." With a smirk, Raphael threw himself into the air, his white wings flapping.

Brody only had eyes for Posie. "I'm sorry I was too late."

"What happens now?" she said, reaching for him again to no avail.

He pulled forth a silken scarf, the magic of it soft and yet firm enough to grasp her soul, allowing him to cradle her after a fashion. "Now I take you for judgment."

19

"JUDGMENT?" The ominous word rang in her head. Wait, did she still technically have a head? Because she remembered what she saw on the pavement. If she still had a stomach, she might have puked. However, she didn't have a belly or a noggin, because she was dead.

By her own choice, too. Heaven sounded like the worst kind of prison, and the angel was talking about a life sentence. Not happening.

Then there was Brody, a man, reaper, whatever, who made her feel. Surely death was preferable to what the angels had in store. She went limp, full-on rag doll, and when Raphael shifted his grip, she twisted hard enough to break free hundreds of feet above the ground. Gravity took hold, and she plummeted.

Landing didn't actually hurt. Too quick and violent for that. What did hurt was the realization she'd lost her chance for a happily ever after. She couldn't believe she couldn't hug Brody.

"What's going to happen to me?" she asked.

"You'll be given a new life in Hell."

"What about..." She glanced at the man who'd hidden his features once more, his cloak drawn low over his face. His sorrow permeated the air. She wished she could touch him one last time. Tell him how she felt, but to say it now...it would only be cruel to them both. Instead she said, "When do we leave?"

"Now." The scarf he'd wrapped around her tugged her as he stepped into that massive nothing place that went on forever and made her feel like the smallest speck of dust.

A second/eternity later they arrived at a crowded dock where shell-shocked people wandered around, eyes wide.

"I can't be dead."

"This isn't Heaven."

"I can't believe that bitch outlived me!"

So many voices mixing into a noisy chaos, and more kept arriving. She saw the swirl of robes here and there as reapers appeared from the nothing place, herding their charges.

Brody kept her wrapped in a silk shroud, tucking

her as close as he could. He shoved through the people, making his way to the flat-bottomed boat tethered at the end of the dock.

A robed figure of a different sort than the reapers stood there, holding on to a long stave that penetrated the dark water. She knew enough about mythology and religion to realize she looked upon the Styx. And that must be Charon, the guy who ferried souls across.

Once she crossed the river, that was it. Life as she knew it truly would be over. Panic filled her. She whirled and tried to grab Brody again. Surely there was something he could—

Her hands passed through him. *No fair.* She would have sobbed if she weren't so angry.

"It will be okay, Posie. Only the truly wicked are punished. You'll be fine," Brody said, his tone low and gravelly.

"You don't know that for sure."

"Given I've been serving for over two hundred years, I have a fair idea."

"Two hundred?" She eyed him. "And how old were you when you died?"

"Young. Which was a problem when I first started working for the Dark Lord. No one takes a fresh-face boy seriously." He rubbed his jaw. "A bargain with a sorceress helped me achieve a more distinguished age."

"Has it been a bad life, since you died?" she asked.

"No. But it hasn't been great either. Actually, until a few weeks ago, it was only about work."

She didn't need him to explain that everything had changed when they met. And now she had to go before they even had a chance together. Who made the stupid rule anyhow that reapers and the souls couldn't get together?

"All aboard!" Charon yelled, ringing a strident bell.

"You have to go."

"Will I ever see you again?" she asked.

"It all depends on the Dark Lord. He's the only one who can help us now." He reached out and ran fingers that passed through her, down her cheek. "Goodbye, my prickly flower."

She found herself standing on the boat, and Brody stepped back on the dock. She almost reached for him as the boat drifted off, but what would be the point? She watched him watching her as they sailed away, ferried across a scary river with eyeballs that popped up for peeks. Tentacles that reached, only to get slapped down by Charon. He wielded his long pole and a shorter stave as extensions of his body. Moving quickly, dazzling those on the boat enough that they forgot they'd died and were going to Hell. A few times they even clapped.

Posie kept an eye for the far shore. It started as a

smudge that evolved into a massive docking area. Not as busy as expected for its size. There were a few flat barges tied to the piers.

A pair of short fellows with webbed fingers and toes scurried out to meet them, securing the ferry and tossing down a gangplank. The souls streamed off and were met by what could only be demons with clipboards. And possibly one vampire, given the human looks and teeth. The souls were separated into groups. Except for Posie.

She stood alone, her name not called, wondering what would happen next.

Then came a shouted, "I'm com-m-m-ing! Out of the way! Oops. I'm sure they can sew that back on." Riding a Segway of all things, a woman in the shortest shorts and a crop top that showed off a naval piercing zipped into view. She zoomed to a stop by Posie and eyed her. "Hello, and welcome to Hell. I am Katie. Also known as Lucifer's Psycho. Nice to meet you." She thrust out a hand, which Posie, bemused, shook.

"How was the ride over? Those sea monsters are playful guys. You like seafood?" Mismatched eyes stared at Posie.

"Um."

"I agree, yum! We should get going. Come on."

Posie found herself being told to grab hold of the

energetic blonde, who kicked the wheeled contraption into gear and off they zoomed.

The only thing to do was absorb as much as she could. Looking around, she noted the city-like aspect, if one ignored the orange hue and the falling ash.

I'm in Hell. It was already stranger than expected. Dangerous, too, given Katie kept tossing knives; left, right, straight ahead. The last leading to a shrill squeak.

After the third, Posie ventured to ask, "Are we safe?"

"Just warning off the rats. We've had some problems with overpopulation since a bunch of our hellcats went missing."

"This looks a lot like Earth," Posie remarked. One that appeared to have suffered some sort of apocalypse.

"In many respects, Hell is a warped mirror of the mortal world, but with more rules to break and less bullshit."

"I guess down here sinning is good."

"Depends on the sin. The truly heinous don't get to live with the general population. The residential areas are reserved for the mundane sinner."

"Am I considered to be a mundane sinner?"

"Obviously not, or you'd already be assigned an apartment. You must have been someone special on

Earth because you are going to court to be judged by the big boss himself," Katie said, jolting the Segway to a stop in front of a massive stone block building that oozed age—and fear.

"What's going to happen to me?"

"Well, that kind of depends on you. If you're truly boring, the Dark Lord might offer to let you exist much like you did when you were alive."

"Or?"

"If you can't handle the heat, you can choose to be reincarnated."

"Are those the only options?"

Katie paused at the bottom of some grand steps and cocked her head. "If you're the type who likes to be busy, there is a third thing you can do that will guarantee an eternity of fun."

"What?"

"Sell your soul to the Devil."

With that shocking suggestion, Katie bounced up the pitted steps showing concrete patches of varying shades. An old edifice that had seen more than its fair share of repairs.

Katie paused to call over her shoulder. "You coming, or planning to be late for your sentencing?"

Posie hurried up the steps. "I want a chance to speak for myself."

"Then you'd better hurry," Katie sang, bolting ahead and out of sight.

Posie quickly followed and soon found herself in a strange but familiar place. A coliseum of sorts, ringed with seats, filled to the brim with everything from humans to monsters, whispering and grunting, quieting as they saw her arrive. Her gaze skimmed over a massive dais holding the most ostentatious throne built of bones. It shimmered as if from intense heat.

Where was the Devil? Would it kill him to be on time?

She tapped her foot impatiently.

A dead silence filled the air as the air in the arena visibly shivered. Someone sneezed, and she automatically said, "Bless you."

"What the fuck? Watch your language. We have younglings in the crowd."

In the blink of an eye, a handsome man suddenly appeared on the raised throne. He casually lounged, his eyes alight with flames, his grin rakish, his crown a molten metal that rippled and roiled atop his head.

"Lucifer…" The name slipped from her lips.

As if he heard the whisper, he winked. "In the lovely flesh. Greetings, Posie Ringwald. Welcome to Hell."

"Hell. Hell. Hell." The crowed stomped and chanted.

She hugged herself as reality intruded. "I shouldn't be here."

"Isn't that what they all say?" Lucifer shook his head.

"I mean it wasn't my time to die, but I had no choice. I was tricked by an angel."

The man on the throne arched a brow. "Tricked? The report filed by the angels say you fell. Are you trying to claim Raphael intentionally dropped you? Because that would be murder and I'd love to nail one of those cocky bastards with that charge."

"No, he didn't drop me, but he was taking me to heaven."

Lucifer visibly shuddered. "I can see why you jumped. Horrible place. All that perfect sunshine, never-changing temps. Not that you would have seen much of it. They're very particular about their humans. And I can't see them being too welcoming of a sinner."

"Excuse me? I'm not bad person," she exclaimed.

"According to my file on you"—a folder appeared in his hand—"you've sinned. Not gregariously. Uncharitable words and thoughts, although I am willing to forgive the insults to the angels. They deserved them. You once kicked a girl in grade three for sneezing on your lunch."

She blinked. She'd forgotten about that. "It was leftover pizza day, and she loogied it."

"You're passive-aggressive with your insults.

Lucky for you, I admire that in the Canadians. Happy bunch, but fuck me, they apologize a lot."

"I'm sorry."

"See what I mean?" He ducked to peruse her file again. "Last place of employment, Grim Dating. Pity we had to lose you. I heard great things." He slapped the folder shut. "Minor shit. We'll have a mundane job and living quarters found for you."

"That's it? I just get to have a new life in Hell?"

"What did you expect? Whips and chains? If we tortured for minor infractions, what would we do for the really big stuff? Isn't it bad enough you get to return to your dull existence?"

"What if I don't want what you're offering?"

Lucifer leaned forward. "You're in Hell. What makes you think you have a choice?"

She remembered Katie's words. He'd offered the mundane. She didn't want to reincarnate, which left only one option.

"I'd like to make a deal."

20

IT JUST ABOUT KILLED BRODY FOR a second time to watch Posie leave on that boat. What would happen to her on the other side? He wished he could have followed, or at least been there by her side, but reapers were forbidden from interfering with souls once they crossed the Styx.

But this wasn't just any soul.

This was Posie. A woman that had captivated him since their first meeting. Someone he'd wanted to have a chance to get to know.

A woman he could love…

He blinked. What happened to love being a lie? A sham? Hadn't he experienced it firsthand? But a betrayal in his past didn't mean he should never love again.

What irony that by the time he finally realized it, he'd lost it.

He could only hope Posie received a light sentence and would find some semblance of happiness. He, on the other hand, would mope for an eternity.

The jostling on the dock had him stepping through a rip in the space between dimensions for a cold, sulky trek back to his office. The bottle of scotch he kept in the drawer might be able to warm him. If he drank the whole thing.

He slammed the bottle on the desk and splashed a generous helping into a glass before he threw himself in his seat. If only there was a way for them to be together. Perhaps if he hung up his cloak? Would the Devil agree to reverse their agreement?

He took a sip. It might be worth a try.

But what if he gave up his cloak and Posie didn't want him anymore?

He couldn't spend the rest of his unlife being afraid of trying. He quickly fired off an email to Lucifer's secretary, requesting an audience. Hopefully, it wouldn't take more than a few months. Years if the Devil didn't want to deal with him.

He poured another drink after he sent the request.

"Drinking so early in the day? It's not even nine a.m. I totally approve."

Lucifer's sudden appearance had him choking and gasping as his sip of scotch went down the wrong tube. "Dark Lord, what are you doing here?"

"You asked for an appointment."

"I— That was rather prompt."

"You mean unpredictable." The Devil winked. "But your email isn't the only reason I'm here. I wanted to tell you in person that there are going to be some changes around here. Big changes."

"I see." Meaning Brody would most likely be fired for failing to win the bet. If only he'd had more time.

With this disgrace hanging over him, could he still convince the Devil to renegotiate his contract?

"Do you see? Because I am still surprised. I mean I knew when I saw her that she'd be a tough nut to crack. The best kind. I thought I had her pinned, ready to take my punishment, when suddenly I found myself more or less grabbed by the balls and squeezed. No wonder you've got the hots for her."

"What are you talking about?" Because Brody couldn't follow.

"Your wench. What a wily female. It's that whole Canadian vibe. Completely throws you off. One minute you think you're putting her in her place, and the next, she's politely insulting you, then apologizing, then making demands, and when it's all over, you realize you've signed the shittiest contact ever."

Did he dare hope? "You're talking about Posie. What happened? Did she make a bargain with you?"

"Did she ever. The wench gave me her soul, kind of, except it's not really mine. It's complicated. Suffice it to say, you'll be working closely with her, so here's to hoping you can tolerate each other."

"Posie is coming back!" he exclaimed.

"She's already here," Lucifer announced, tipping back the whiskey and guzzling it.

Posie stepped out of nowhere, looking a tad uncertain, but her smile as she saw him was wide. "Hi, Brody."

"Posie?" He didn't dare believe she was actually here. "Is it really you?" Despite the fear he'd run right through her, he vaulted his desk, his robe flaring behind him, hands reaching, only to pause at the last moment. Fearful. What if he couldn't touch her?

She grabbed his hands. "It's me. I'm really here."

"But how?" It was then he paid attention to her outfit. Shaped as a dress, the fabric appeared to be the same as his garment, yet molded to fit her like real clothes would—in a deep red.

"Are you?"

"A reaper? Not exactly. I'll never collect souls."

"Her job is actually going to be matching them." Lucifer rubbed his hands. "Think of her as Cupid 2.0."

She winced. "Can we not call it that?"

"Given you got paid vacation and sick days, I will damned well call it whatever I fucking like," Lucifer huffed with a sulfurous breath.

"Your wife must be something special having to deal with three children at home."

"Two... Aha, I see what you did there." Lucifer wagged a finger. "Like I said, those Canadians are sly. But reliable. I'll expect great things from your office."

Brody would ensure the very best if it meant having Posie by his side. He couldn't stop staring at her. "I can't believe you're here."

"Yeah, well, I can't believe it all turned out to be real. I just wish I hadn't taken so long to believe. Guess my picture will be beside the definition of stubborn."

"Right beside mine because of how long it took me to admit what you mean to me. I love you, Posie Ringwald. Especially when you're a wily Canuck."

Her lips twitched. "And I love you even if you look like death."

Lucifer gagged. "Fuck me, would you stop it already? Disgusting. I'm leaving."

"Gaia's calling you," Posie remarked, cocking her head.

"She is not. I'm leaving 'cause I want to," Lucifer huffed.

"She said to grab a pack of diapers from the store on your way home."

"I know. I know. And some more teething gel. Bloody antichrist is rough on the skin." Lucifer held up a bruised wrist and grimaced.

Snap.

The Lord of the Underworld left, and Brody could finally do the thing he'd been dying to since he saw Posie.

Kiss her thoroughly.

EPILOGUE

A FEW WEEKS LATER...

"Morning, lover," Posie murmured from the combined cocoon of their robes. It formed a warm layer over their naked bodies, a built-in blanket that never let them feel the cold.

"Hello," he rumbled, his hands skimming over her naked flesh.

"We should get up," she declared. "We need to shower before work."

"You and your sense of responsibility," he grumbled. "Why can't we sleep in?"

"Because it's not sleep you're looking for, but sex."

"Can't I have sex then a nap?"

She laughed. "No. We have a job to do."

"My job is to make you happy." He nuzzled her neck, proving yet again how good he was at that task.

"I really shouldn't be skipping days given I'll need to take some time off in about eight months."

He froze. "You're pregnant? How is that possible?" Because while a Grim could impregnate a human or demon, they couldn't procreate with each other. A bit of a failsafe built into the magic to ensure the reapers didn't take over the world.

"Apparently it happened before I died, and when the Devil put me back in my body, he left it there."

His eyes widened, and he placed his hand on her belly. "A child."

"Our child."

"A minion for my army!" Lucifer declared, suddenly appearing at the end of the bed, his son sitting on his shoulders, chubby fists knotted in his father's hair. The Devil also held a swaddled baby in his arms, the blanket pink and covered in sloths with giant grins.

But that wasn't the strangest thing. Posie blinked, and yet the image didn't leave.

"What's wrong?" Brody hissed, noticing her silence while the Devil narrowed his gaze.

How could she explain to Brody that while Lucifer appeared as he usually did—a very handsome, yet slightly menacing man with the biggest, blackest wings, and his son, a miniature of him, with a smaller pair and little horns—the baby in his arms was—

Projectile puking!

Screaming as it hit, Posie rolled out of bed with Brody following suit as the Devil's smallest child proved it had a stomach filled in another dimension.

By the time Posie was done heaving and then showering, she'd forgotten what she'd seen.

Lucifer made sure of it.

———

JUNIOR WENT DOWN FOR HIS NAP, MEANING LUCIFER had only Jujube to deal with. Not the baby's actual name, but the one he liked best given she looked like a bonbon. Pink and delicious.

He held her in front of him and crooned, "Who's my sweet baby girl? Who's going to love her mama forever and ever and never kill her?"

The baby cooed and shook her chubby fists, reaching for him. She grabbed his beard and yanked.

"Gentle, tiny princess."

She hiccupped, and all the hair on his face evaporated.

He blinked.

She blinked. Burped and farted. Before going to sleep.

Very much Daddy's girl. Boy was the world fucked.

NOT EVEN CLOSE TO THE END OF THIS SERIES...

GET READY FOR SPARKS TO FLY IN SWEEPING ASHLEY. CAN A GRUFF REAPER sweep a tidy witch off her feet?

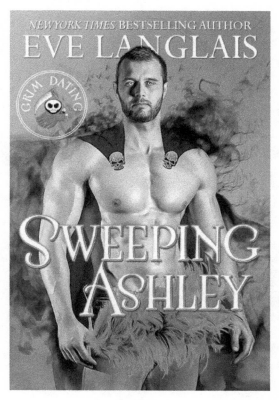

For more stories please see http://www.EveLanglais.com

Newsletter: http://evelanglais.com/newrelease

CPSIA information can be obtained
at www.ICGtesting.com
Printed in the USA
LVHW032109290421
685986LV00011B/1454